Chance For Love
Sexy Stories Collection

VOLUME 15

10 EROTIC SHORT STORIES

BREANA KOHR

Chance For Love/ Breana Kohr. -- 1st ed.
Xplicit Press, an imprint of TLM Media LLC

ISBN-13: 978-1-62327-546-4
ISBN-10: 1-62327-546-6
eISBN: 978-1-62327-596-9

Printed in the United States of America

CONTENTS

1   The End To Wifey's Jealousy   1

2   A Mermaid's Love   19

3   Whoops Looks Like We Wandered Into A Sex Club   33

4   A Second Chance For Love   49

5   Sexy Alien Prison Breaks   63

6   The Greatest Test of a Man's Love   79

7   The First Love Spell I Cast   97

8   My Affair With An American Eccentric   117

9   Meet and Ditch   135

10   The Life My Master Allows Me   151

1 THE END TO WIFEY'S JEALOUSY

The green-eyed monster never sleeps. No matter who a man talks to, whether it's a friend, a coworker, or even a family relative. Rest assured, Wifey is always there scouting out her competition. My theory is that women understand the psyche of men very well. They know we think about fucking every woman we see—not just a little, but a lot—as in thinking of what positions would work and how we could set up a secret hotel meeting without arousing suspicion.

A woman's instinct is to quickly subdue the threat, either by pointing out how ugly the other woman is or imply that she's a good for nothing whore not worth her husband's time. Blame the female's desire to keep her man controlled on evolutionary disposition. We hunt, and they protect the home. Don't blame me for being a sexist pig, blame God. Or better yet, blame the evolution that made us that way.

I don't ever take shit from my woman, and I think it's about time men start acting like men and take back control of their sexual desires. I pride myself on being a man of temptation, short moral scruples, and living dangerously. I've always said that I never cheat on the woman I'm with, and I have never lied about that.

Of course, that doesn't mean I've suffered through monogamy or celibacy in all my 36 years of life on this amazing planet. My first wife, Marilyn, and I were swingers, and fidelity was never an issue. She and I both had a raging libido and agreed that if we had sex with other people, we would have to share them.

After we broke up, I got together with Lizzy, and we experimented with an open marriage. We slept with whomever we wanted but always came back home to tell each other stories, watch movies, and eat really good Cajun food.

I do think all good things must come to an end, which explains why those relationships never worked out. Still, I made it a point to tell Helen, my third wife, that I am always faithful, but horny as a dog. She said she was "okay with it," but as I figured, she was lying to herself, trying so hard to tame that green-eyed beast that lurks inside all beautiful things.

Helen is beautiful, no doubt. If I believed in monogamy, I would probably end up with her cute little tush anyway. She's young, in her late twenties, and with adorable brown bangs on top of her long straight hair. She's young, all right, but tight-assed in both good and bad ways. She is insanely jealous of my time and hates how easily I flirt with beautiful women. I've been blessed with good looks, a tall stature, and a high degree of self-confidence. I don't really know what it feels like to deprive myself of good things.

Helen loves my "tall, dark" disposition, with my black hair and deep eyes. Yeah, that's what women always say. They talk about the eyes and the dimples and the gentle soul. Trust me though - it doesn't hurt that I have chiseled abs, tight pecks, a supple and squeezable ass, and a nine-inch dick. Even though women won't say it, we all know they think about it!

I had a long talk with Helen a few months ago, discussing her obsessive jealousy. I felt the world closing in on me as she tried to inch her way towards a monogamous relationship with me—a rather dreary existence, all things considered.

The best course of action was the gentle but direct opposition. I called her on her prudish attitude and asked why faithfulness had to be so boring. She fumed, of course, letting off some steam, which I imagine is all related to her low self-image.

She wants to force me to be faithful because she can't fathom herself having affairs with other people. I encouraged her to go out and satisfy her curiosity, and feel the wonderful difference an open marriage brings you.

Helen calmed down eventually and tried to see things from a rational point of view.

"I am so jealous of you. I know it's obsessive, but I just don't want to lose you, Daryl."

"You're never going to lose me, baby. When I married you, I agreed to be with you forever, but I never agreed to stop having fun. Wherever I go, I want to take you with me. But I think along the way to our ultimate destination, we shouldn't be afraid to try new things."

We talked about hypothetical situations all night long. She admitted that she would like to sample some guys she knew. She admitted the idea of a threesome with two men sounded intriguing. However, to my disappointment, she didn't express any secret lesbian longing.

Still, real progress has been made, and I was proud of myself for sticking to my guns and not falling into the trap of monogamy.

"I don't want you to think I'm a prude," Helen said to me, thinking over our options. "I know some of it is low self-esteem or whatever ... and I don't want to be an eighty-year-old lady someday, who missed out on all of these opportunities. I want to experience everything with you ..."

She said this as we made love that night, thinking of other people and embracing a new challenge in our relationship. I told her my fantasy later on. She asked me to be brutally honest and say everything I was thinking: who I wanted to fuck, how I wanted to fuck them, and old friends of ours I secretly wanted to fuck but never told her.

There were no big surprises, although I was amused to know my wife was attracted to a black friend of mine. I told her, "Believe me, Gregg will always be there for you, because you have one gorgeous, ghetto booty."

We laughed the night away, eager to see where our sordid fantasies would take us. Then I unloaded a bombshell on her, one that I wasn't sure she was ready for. But hey, she asked for it, right?

I told her about my smoking hot

secretary Nonique, a young Latina woman who I flirted with at the office. I admitted not only that I wanted to sleep with her but also that she was more than willing. The only catch is that Nonique is a good girl and doesn't want to be a labeled as a home wrecker. But, as she once explained to me at lunch, all is fair game when Wifey is there.

I told this to my wife and she almost lapsed into prudery again, lashing out at poor little Nonique for daring to volunteer her service. Still, Helen was determined to prove herself as a confident, sexy woman not confined by sexual boundaries. She asked for me to take photos of Nonique so that she could see why I wanted her so badly.

Nonique was exotically gorgeous. She had straight long black hair and a perfectly tight body, with a firm ass and two perky C-cup tits. She was a good girl but she wasn't above wearing sexy clothes to the office: we're talking tight skirts, high heels, and a "professional" work shirt that she wore unbuttoned just so we could gaze at her cleavage in secret. Her face was somewhat innocent, which is another reason I had to show her to Helen. Despite having dark and mordant eyes, she had a very playful disposition and a bit of a goofy-looking grin.

When my wife saw Nonique's picture

she admitted that she was beautiful. After agreeing to some terms (actually, a lengthy contract), she said she would let me sleep with her, but only if she could be in the same room while it happened. Hopefully that wasn't a bluff, because I was on the phone with Nonique within minutes, arranging our first after-hours office date.

My wife was nervous for the day of the meeting, so I arranged to have her talk to Nonique on the phone, just to let her know what was going to happen.

"Hiii!" Nonique said, excited and giggly. "Is this Helen?"

"Hi there," Helen said back mirroring her giggly and nervous disposition.

"So ... you know about Daryl's proposition?"

"Yes. Yes, I think I do," Helen replied unsurely.

"Don't be nervous," she cooed. "It will be okay. It will be fun."

"Fun, huh? So what's going to happen exactly?" Helen asked nervously.

"Well ... uh ..." she laughed again. "You know!"

"No, tell me!" Both girls giggled, enjoying their newfound intimacy.

"Well ... I'm thinking maybe some dim lights ... a few drinks ..."

"Mmm-hmm," Helen mumbled, her green eyes flashing in anticipation.

"Then we tie you up. And you watch

Daryl and me together."

Helen opened her eyes in surprise. Nonique's thick Latina accent was a huge turn on for me, and I could tell she was provoking Helen already. This was going to be beautiful.

Helen and I dressed up for the event. She wore a pink sweater and a black skirt, while I sported a dark blue sports coat and pants. We arrived at my office afterhours, when it was completely dark and quiet—the perfect setting for a naughty fantasy to come to life. We waited impatiently for Nonique to come back after going home to "freshen up."

When she arrived, she was truly a knockout, wearing a sexy low-cut black blouse with long straps, a black skirt, and a vinyl belt. We didn't just jump into wild sex, of course. We had to stew a little bit. We had some drinks, giggled at our own naughty minds, and played one round of truth or dare.

By Nonique's fourth glass of sherry, she was flying and decided to move things along. She asked my wife a bold question.

"Soo ... have you ever been with another girl?"

"No." Helen answered abruptly. "I'm just taking baby steps, according to Daryl's plan."

"Oh, I *see*. You like to watch?" Nonique asked provokingly, gauging Helen's level of resentment and kink.

"I don't know ... yet," Helen replied cautiously.

Nonique looked at me, indicating that it was time to begin our game. She took my wife by the hand, raising her off of the couch and leading her to my desk chair.

Nonique gently sat my wife down on the chair and lifted her arms into position. She brought out a pair of wrist restraints from her purse and attached them to the arm bars and around Helen's dainty little wrists.

She made sure Helen was tightly affixed to that chair, so tight that she couldn't even budge. I don't know if this was a power trip or if she was really afraid of Helen jumping up and killing her, but I checked over her restraints and knew there was no chance of Helen breaking free.

Nonique slowly walked over to our hostage, getting familiar with the moment and enjoying the tingling sensation. Helen shifted uncomfortably, not sure what was coming next.

The stranger's voice dropped a notch as she stared my wife straight in the eyes. "You like to watch your husband with other girls?" She laughed while Helen stared back at her.

Nonique turned to me and put her arms around my back. She gave me a luscious French kiss, making sure my significant other heard every last smacking detail. It felt so vividly wrong, another woman's tongue in my mouth while my helpless wife watched. This was going to get so much worse before it got better.

I started kissing my sexy friend's long and dainty neck, breathing down her cleavage, ready to taste her forbidden fruits. Nonique was definitely excited and exaggerated her sighs, knowing they were affecting my wife, who glared at us. She didn't have any hate in her eyes, or even any sadness. She simply watched. Maybe she was enjoying it. Maybe she was planning to kill us tomorrow. Whatever it was, I couldn't stop now.

I put my lips to Nonique's full and supple breasts, my lips softly smothering her chest, wanting to suck hard on those brown and tangy nipples. She backed away so I could watch her take that tight blouse off without any obstacles. My God, were her tits beautiful. She didn't wear a bra to our little outing. As soon as she lifted up that blouse, her gorgeous tits came tumbling down, bouncing around me, bare as can be and calling my name. Without even looking at Helen for permission, I ransacked Nonique's tits, gobbling up her erect nipples and squeezing her fleshy chest with my hungry hands.

I sensed my wife shifting around. It was getting to her. I could stop right now. I could give this up, take her back home, apologize, and retreat back to a course of happy monogamy. That was one option. Or I could fuck the brains out of Nonique, my knock-out Latina treasure, while my wife watched.

I decided to go with the second option.

I sat Nonique on my desk and made sure my nervous wife got a full view of what was to come. My hand meandered up to this sweetheart's pussy. Even through her red panties, I could feel how wet she was.

"You want me to fuck you?" I asked Nonique.

"Yeah," she swooned, looking up at me from the desk like a wild child ready to cause a scene. We both looked back at Helen, not asking permission, but making sure she saw every last detail of our time together.

I unbuttoned my pants as Nonique slid off her underwear. Enjoying a wild streak, the little vixen threw her soaked panties in my wife's direction, just so she could more closely smell the scent of her pussy.

"You liking this, hon?" Nonique called over to Helen who was still eerily silent.

I went closer to the desk and shoved my hard cock into this little miss's pussy. Oh God, was her pussy tight!

"Oh, yeah! Yeah! Give it to me!" Nonique started chanting as I railed her back and forth, so relieved to fuck freely again, to feel the loss of control, and to follow my inhibitions. All Helen could see was my butt humping in the air and Nonique's topless figure writhing to the beat. But she knew exactly what I knew: there was no giving up this ultra-tight wet pussy. I couldn't help but scream in agony, inches away from having the cumshot of the century.

I was ready to come but I stopped myself for the grand finale. Nonique and I stopped mid-fuck just so we could pay the old green-eyed monster a visit.

Helen started to tense up as she saw a dick and two bare tits wandering in her direction.

"What ... what? What are you doing?"

"Surprise, honey," I said with a devious smile. Did you really think that we were going to let you watch without participating? It's just rude not to entertain your host."

"No wait ... wait ..."

Nonique ignored Helen's bitching and started unbuttoning her pretty pink sweater. Helen shifted around, feeling something intense, but not admitting it. I think it was just the site of Nonique's huge tits right in front of her face ... that, and the wonderful feeling of having another women strip you down naked. Helen objected, but they were soft, naughty sort of objections. I think she was enjoying the erotic moment and wanted to feel how Nonique made me feel. Well, she was in luck, because that's precisely what we decided to give her.

My girlfriend unbuttoned my wife's sweater blouse all the way to the bottom, exposing her beautiful black bra. Helen's tits are nothing to take for granted. They're not big and bopping like Nonique's, but she has incredibly thick nipples and a wonderful fleshly shape.

Our Spanish beauty queen kneeled down in front of my beloved's chair and poked around under her dress.

"Mmmm!" Helen purred aloud, probably ashamed to be so turned on.

She put her hand deeper inside, touching my wife's pussy hair and feeling her walls, pushing her slender fingers in and out of that spongy chamber.

"You like being touched that way, huh?" she said harshly, while she oh-so-gently massaged her clit.

Both women were wet and I was in heaven, smelling their essence and watching one beautiful woman make finger love to another.

"Look at me," Nonique barked at my shivering wife. She grabbed her embarrassed little face with her left hand, just a bit roughly, while she put her lovely fingers up my wife's slippery slope.

"Ahhh ... " my beloved moaned as the strange young vixen dug even deeper.

Nonique then increased the finger speed, inserting two fingers in deep and then back out again. She hit the G-spot perfectly because within seconds my lovely wife was crying out. "Oh fuck! Fuck!" she yelled out, as Nonique finger-fucked her with rage. "Oh right there, right there!"

She squirmed all over the seat, still being tightly confined by the unforgiving restraints. This bodacious brunette was coming so hard she was shaking the chair and giving Nonique's hand a free massage.

"Ohh! Ohhh!" she bellowed with uninhibited noise, her eyes rolling in the back of her head and making all kinds of funny gag faces.

"So ... you still think the G-spot is a myth?" I had to ask with a chortle.

"Oh fuck no! Oh! Oh ... I'm coming again!"

I sunk my hands into my wife's bra, squeezing her hidden nipples. It was a great rhythmic aftershock to join her unwilling orgasm.

I called out words of encouragement to the dame with the magic hands. "Come on, Nonique! Pound that pussy! Fuck it like you mean it!"

She listened to me and followed orders with zest, increasing the speed and letting us all hear what pussy swiping sounds like.

"Ooooh!" Helen shrieked, throwing her head back and taking that G-spot pounding like a champion.

My new girlfriend and I quieted down, enjoying Helen's basking afterglow and panting breaths. She didn't say anything … probably because she had just been finger-fucked royally by a smoking hot, bare-chested beauty!

Helen, trying to recover from a full body orgasm, could barely look Nonique in the eye. But the black-haired vamp invaded Helen's territory again and got right in her face. She enjoyed the role a little too much and seemed to get a kinky thrill out of seeing my wife's squinted green eyes and gritting teeth.

"Let me out," Helen ordered.

I was willing to let my beloved out of her shackles, as she proved herself a great sport. But that kinky little Spanish demon had something else on her mind. Jesus! I'll say one thing; single women with "morals" are into some kinky shit just as long as nobody's lying about it!

"Put her on the floor," she commanded, eyeing my wife in her helpless state.

"What ... what are you doing?"

"Don't talk back!" she yelled. "Do what I say. I'm fucking your husband, not you."

Before Helen could shoot her a dirty look, I had already taken my cue and carefully tipped the chair over, slowly lowering my tied up wife gently down to the floor. Her shoulders lay on the back of the chair, while her legs were up in the air, flailing like crazy, but unable to save her, since her arms were immobilized.

"Daryl! What are you doing?"

"It's not over yet, honey," I said with a gentle touch to her chin, "Just let go. Let it happen."

Nonique came over to my upside down wife and assumed the position. She kneeled down and squirmed her way forward, putting her now bare, dripping pussy all over Helen's tummy and resting her knees outside her abdomen. She bent her head down just enough to reach the green-eyed monster's flowing pussy and buried her pretty face in that mound. All Helen saw, as Nonique prepared her for a third orgasm, was Nonique's perfect ass and waxed little asshole sliding up and down her bellybutton.

The busty brunette I loved could take no more and started howling as her clit was licked up like a lollipop. "Oh God! Daryl! I can't take this again, don't make me come again."

"It's okay, this is the cure for what ails you."

Nonique took a break and spit my wife's taste from her mouth. "Shut her up, Daryl."

Helen looked on in shock as I followed my mistress' suggestion.

I took out my big cock and stuffed it into Helen's gaping mouth hole. "You just take that cock in your mouth and be quiet," I commanded her, face fucking her until she gagged.

The sounds that night were melodious. For hours on end, I heard nothing but my wife gagging, her muffled cock-filled voice probably screaming that she was going to come again, and my girlfriend slurping up my wife's juicy pussy.

Leave it to my lovely and versatile wife to end the perfect night like a drama queen.

By her fourth orgasm, she screamed so loud she just about spit my cock out of her mouth and sang the highest C note I've ever heard.

"Ooooohhhh!" she screamed as she squirted all over Nonique's face.

Nonique, covered in goop, looked over at me and laughed.

"Oh my god..." my wife sighed and repeated her statement again and again for the next ten minutes. Besides all the cumming and fucking, the best part of the night was sitting around naked in the office we usually work from, admiring each other's natural nude forms.

My advice to guys out there with a jealous wife or girlfriend who's questioning your fidelity: just give her multiple orgasms. That's real therapy for you.

2 A MERMAID'S LOVE

Willard knew what they meant when they said the sea was a lady. The sea was temperamental, the sea was beautiful, and the sea nurtured emotional wounds just like a good woman. Was it odd that instead of fantasizing about a quick lay or a naïve college girl, Willard's wet dreams were of the Atlantic Ocean and the Caspian Sea?

Maybe it wasn't what young men yearned for, but for old men like Willard, it was a vivid fantasy, one worth living for, something to look forward to after retirement, and one truly worth dying for. To be buried at sea, to die in the ocean, would be an honor. Whether a man died of starvation, of thirst, or even at the jaws of a shark, to die in the arms of your lover would be an honor.

Willard figured that a life at sea, whether deadly or tranquil, would be a better life than he experienced throughout his fifty years on land. The land aged him, terribly; he hardly even remembered the last twenty years of his life. Failed relationships, clocking in and clocking out, and embarrassing himself chasing after things that weren't his to take.

The old man loved Moby Dick in particular, not just because he related to Ahab's dreams and obsessive quests, but because he admired the fact that Ahab had a purpose. To Willard, the obsession didn't matter; the practicality didn't matter. What mattered was the belief—the belief that it all ends somewhere, for a purpose, it all ends poetically.

The alternative was not so beautiful—working in a fish and tackle store right by the lake, only getting a whiff of the sea's intimate scent, not anywhere near the deep.

"How's the wind today?"

"It's a bit volatile," he said softly to the young lions ready to try their worst at kite surfing.

"We can handle it, Ahab."

"Keep an eye on the place, chief."

Fools. Disrespectful hooligans. They know nothing of the real sea, the real journey. Then again, what did he know? And how long was he to suffer before the "real life" began, out at sea, the watery grave that called him? If only retirement weren't so far away. Fifteen more years of this, he wondered to himself, never pretentious so as to speak his worries aloud, in prudence to the fact someone may have been listening.

Years ago, the old man ceased his ridiculous behavior of courting young lasses and husband-hunters. He didn't have the money to spoil one or the temperament to tame one. They were sharks on land, ruthless, blood hungry, and without fear. Every time a pretty young thing came near Willard, he retreated, like a monster in hiding, like a dolphin escaping a greater predator.

Whenever that painful reminder of old age came upon him, the thought of sunnier days, of relaxing times when there was no such thing as loss or regret, would also come to mind. There were only long weekends of coasting, fishing, and dreaming. Dreaming of uncharted territories, dreaming of what it must have been like generations ago, back when there were undiscovered worlds and where the travelers, the explorers, claimed what they found.

Not like today, when everything is handed to a man, a world in which he pisses where they tell him to piss. Maybe he was doomed to repeat the same day in and day out schedule for another decade. But, to hell with today, he thought to himself, as he closed the shop early.

The boss would be displeased. He would lose a day's wage. But today belonged to his mistress. Her scent was in the air and his tickling fingers were brushing against his white beard with promises of a wet and wondrous journey.

It was a long journey ahead for sure and not the safest idea Willard had ever come up with. He himself didn't know whether he had a death wish, a mental breakdown, or merely an impulsive inclination to taste the mist of open water.

Whatever it was, he abandoned his post and welcomed his fate. He took his crudely built sail boat, the Willard LIT, into the waters and pointed the boat toward the wind. Lacking a wind direction indicator, he had created his own concoction, consisting of several inches of old VHS tape tied to the rigging cables holding up the mast.

Willard didn't know precisely where he was going, but was determined that he was going to let the sea guide him—first to the edge of the lake and then hopefully into the estuary and eventually into the unprotected sea.

He had sailed enough in his time to

know what he was doing was a cry to the great angry mistress; whenever the wind was strong, as in a day much like that day, a lone sailor could be easily overpowered by the wind. Instinct told him that it was time to reef the sail. The wind that day was fuming and his little boat was already in danger of broaching.

At the very least, it was time to put down the anchor. To go against his sailor's instinct would be tempting fate, challenging his Lady. He simply stared out into the open water, as minutes turned into hours, and long after the boat steered off course.

The wind eventually calmed, securing the boat's passage, and allowing Willard to take a long, deserved nap. He let his vessel sail, far, far into uncharted waters, or at least he hoped that he would be, fearing the drudgery of another day on land.

As he flinched in and out of the dream state, he felt an otherworldly presence with him. At first, he believed it to be the sea caressing him into a watery grave. Then, he supposed it was the pangs of madness.

However, as he left the dream state, he noticed the presence growing stronger, as if approaching him inch by inch.

He opened his eyes, still resting his head on an inflatable travel pillow on the floor of the Willard LIT. He quickly shifted his head to the right but saw nothing. Still, the body tingling and the buzzing in the air remained. He quickly turned to his left.

There he beheld: a woman of the sea— physical manifestation of the harsh lover that called to him.

Her hair was deep, dark blue and her complexion was fair, pale, and almost translucent and glowing, as if an aquatic creature from the deep.

Willard jumped back, startled at what he thought he saw, and the creature disappeared instantly, leaving behind a splashing sound below.

He sat up quickly, analyzing the water, trying to figure out what images he saw and what might have been imagined.

He decided to play dead a moment, leaning back against the pillow and shutting his eyes. He made sure whatever it was saw his calm and relaxed breathing rate. Just as with catching a fish, he lured it out, seducing it into a falsely secure environment.

When he slowly opened his eyes, he saw it again: a ghostly but beautiful complexion staring down at him. As its eyes widened, upon realizing it had been seen, Willard quickly spoke up, raising his pitch but slowing down his pace.

"Don't be afraid!" He reassured the escaping human-like creature that was still a world away in form. "I just want to see you. I won't hurt you."

The creature came back up from the water but from the opposite end of the boat, a comfortable distance from Willard's threatening arms.

The creature rose slowly and gave Willard a startling view of its body. Willard's guest was female in form with long, stringy hair that looked as dark as night in the dusk sky. She had a feminine face with pouty lips and a natural face—except for one feature: her unusually large and playful eyes.

The she-demon had pasty skin but beautiful bare breasts far too supple to be covered by her hair. Her nipples were slightly green but still reminded the old man of young, fertile women back in the day.

"I...I have never seen anything like you," Willard said in his soft voice, which the sea creature found to be peaceable. "Can you understand me? What I am saying?"

She tilted her head to him, much like a sea lion might reply to a trainer.

"No...of course not. But you understand my tone. You know that I'm not going to hurt you."

She tilted her head again.

"I wonder...I wonder if you would mind showing me the rest of you?"

He thought it over a moment, realizing

the quizzical-faced creature was trying to understand his feelings, not his words.

He gestured for the womanly being to come aboard his sail ship, flailing his arms and pointing. She hesitated for a moment, looking into his face, and trying to decipher his motivations. He continued pointing at the boat and making peaceable sounds.

The sea lady finally got the idea and briskly jumped into the sail boat, almost tipping the vessel over.

Willard laughed and reassured his guest all was well with his smile. He looked on in astonishment as he saw the true nature of his visitor. She had a human torso and breasts, but the lower extremities of a large barracuda. With his calm and entreating body language, he asked to touch her scales. She cautiously let him caress her tail, her fins, and her little blowhole on the backside of her figure. For a moment, Willard wondered if the blowhole was the mermaid version of the female sex organ, or if it merely operated as a means of expelling air and breathing. She didn't seem to inhale or exhale and yet she seemed perfectly at peace on the boat or inside the water.

He poked the blowhole with his finger to which the female tittered, making a jubilant face. He smiled back at her and the girl's fish tail flapped around, as if cooing in delight.

Her breasts exposed to him and her face looking so divinely human and innocent, the dreaming sailor felt great temptation. Everything about the woman was alluring and not only her shapely figure, but also her fins, seemed curiously erotic. He tried to fight the feeling, reminding his weary lust that she was naïve and probably underdeveloped, at least in fish years. Still, with the body of a busty college girl and the exotic features of a goddess, Willard's self-control was waning.

The mermaid started to glance at Willard's tired face in aggressive curiosity, invading his space and capriciously poking his nose. When she came too close to his face, he gently but firmly took her by the head and planted a hairy old kiss on her lips.

The mermaid shot her eyes open and she flapped her fin around in alarm, grabbing the sailboat edges and preparing to jump out.

"I'm sorry!" he cried out, seeing that his stolen kiss scared her. "I-I didn't mean to startle you," he said, showing his palms and tilting his head in apology.

The mermaid moved her head sideways, examining Willard one suspicious eye at a time. The mermaid slithered her body closer toward him and began to once again invasively analyze him. She touched his face and put her hand on his shirt.

As if offended at Willard's deception, the mermaid became agitated and grabbed Willard's shirt.

"Hey!"

She ripped fabric apart and threw the remains out to sea.

"Don't do that!" he scolded her.

"Hsssss!" she warned him, as her eyes lost their pupils and began to glow in rage.

"Now calm down...no harm was meant. They're just clothes. No disguises. You see?"

A shirtless Willard slid off his shorts, leaving his briefs on, which the fish girl inspected closely.

"Be careful now..."

The child-like creature noticed the bulge in the sailor's pants and couldn't help but discover what other strange treasures the man hid from her. She reached into the folds of his briefs with her squirming hands until she found something fleshy and taut.

To her astonishment, she brought out a moccasin-like appendage from the man's pants, which seemed to grow in her hand. She looked carefully at its veins and its prick hole, which she likely thought was a breathing apparatus.

"Oh, child..." the excited Willard exclaimed, as the miraculous sea woman squeezed his erect member causing it to bulge and shake. "Wait...wait..." he said, trying to back away from her and spare her the humiliation of an old man's broken rod.

The creature hissed again, apparently demanding submission from its captive new friend.

The mermaid looked at his raging flagpole one more time and then decided to lick it with her long, lizard-like tongue.

"Oh..." Willard cried with a heavy breath. "I don't think you know what you're doing..."

The mermaid looked at him in warning, with a face that almost felt like sadism, if only the young creature knew what all of these emotions really encompassed.

She watched his eyes in caution as she stuffed the meaty harpoon into her mouth. She tasted its leakage and licked up all of its salty nuances. She alternated between licking it, sucking it in, and blowing it out as if to inflate its size (alas, to no avail).

All the variations felt fantastic to the old sailor who was reminded of both the beauty of human copulation and the wondrous fishy smell of sex.

The old man in the sea came close to ejaculating and tried to warn his mysterious lover by waving and tapping his hands. The mermaid only sucked harder the more Willard objected, all the while keeping her beady eyes and suddenly empty expression focused on him.

As Willard began to fire his canons, the mermaid flipped her tail repeatedly on the floor of the boat, as if to summon enough strength and leverage to her mouth being occupied. Willard strained as he unloaded himself into the mermaid's mouth, lacking the incredible staying power of yesterday.

There was no time for peaceful afterglow, however; immediately after taking his sperm in her mouth, her cheeks puffed up to abnormal size. She was orally storing his indecencies but for what sinister purpose?

Willard slowly faded in and out of consciousness for the next few hours, all the while hearing strange singing sensations and consistent voice echoes.

After falling asleep, Willard awoke to see a particularly disturbing site: hundreds of eggs sitting inside the sailboat and with a big-cheeked fish girl ready to spew onto them.

He looked away from the grotesque site but knew precisely what was happening. She had taken on the mating habits of clownfish and only desired human sperm for her egg fertilization.

Willard contemplated interspecies dating and the mermaid's true motivation for seducing him—perhaps a rebellion against the sea kingdom underwater? And more importantly, he worried, would this rebellion summon Poseidon himself and lead to a great war?

Till today, Willard's whereabouts remain a mystery. A few of Willard's friends continue to spread the rumors that a mermaid kidnapped him and killed him. Others believe he escaped her clutches but drowned at sea, while still others believe he went to join the fish woman creature and live in her own magical kingdom.

Whatever the fate of Willard, not a man on land feels pity for him. He lusted after the great woman of the sea and has only himself to blame for welcoming her fury.

3 WHOOPS LOOKS LIKE WE WANDERED INTO A SEX CLUB

"We're new to this."
"Yeah...this is our first time."
"Just lurking. Not doing."
"Yes, very shy. Just here to watch."
We said this from the very beginning. And whenever we said it, we would always be greeted by a host of giggles, funny stares, and knowing smiles. Truthfully, it was our first time and we never intended it to go...umm, how shall we say, this far?

So we were, Mark and Meryl, the traditional working class couple, reaching that dreadful point in our lives where we needed to "spice up" our marriage. Things were pretty good between us actually. We had sex once a week. We were in pretty good shape if I say so myself. My husband has a nice figure and is tall, handsome, and very seductive in the way he talks. I am the brainy working housewife, complete with executive glasses, straight black hair, and a naturally firm physique that comes from a full-time job and taking care of my horses for hours on end on weekends. And when I say "take care," believe me, nothing funny is going on. Mostly scooping up manure and feeding the bratty creatures.

So it wasn't really ignorance or gullibility holding us back. We each had our own collection of sex toys. We would both look at porn on the Internet. Sure, we each had our own secret Internet cybersex partner, you know, the "friend" whom we always seemed to be talking to all day for no apparent reason.

But our sex life wasn't really lacking. It's just that we didn't do all the Tantra stuff or the obligatory threesome. Besides, we were never really the prudish couple that got all hot and bothered ordering a sex toy sampler kit from "Adam and Eve." I mean hell, I had gone through more vibrators in a year than my husband did Fleshlights. Sex toys just weren't that spicy.

So what is left for a jaded couple like us to experience?

While vacationing in Sydney last year,

we came across a rather seedy strip club. The hostess who was standing outside and handing out fliers seemed nice and perky, so we decided to go inside and see what was so hot about naked Aussie titties. While we were both amused at the idea of going into a strip club, the actual show seemed kind of depressing. A cute skinny girl got on stage and barely danced, and she was received coldly by the spoiled patrons. Out of pity, Mark gave her a C-note, as if to assure her to keep trying 'cause you will be an awesome stripper some day!

So the strip club was definitely a downer. I came up with the brilliant idea of attending a live sex show. Of course, the only advertised live sex shows are in Amsterdam, Barcelona, and Israel. Everywhere else you go, you get either strippers or "lurkers" in an unofficial adult movie hangout.

Here's the thing about the adult movie hangout. They don't officially allow live sex but it always happens. This we knew, so we wanted to watch—you know, to experience something new. Unfortunately, we vacationed in Grainerville, the weirdest fucking town in California, and got way more than we bargained for.

When we first arrived at the club, we were greeted by the most unwelcoming and stuffy bouncers I had ever seen. They seemed less like snotty bouncers and more like resentful Secret Service men. We were actually dressed fairly well, and I was a knockout in my black strapless chiffon dress and A-line skirt.

When we were let inside, we were not given any seats or any directions on what room to enter for the movie. There were a few actually. We attempted to circulate and talk to other visitors, but to our alarm, everyone there seemed a bit spacy (drunk, maybe?) and downright goofy (like pothead giggly).

Mark became annoyed right about the time the fifth girl laughed at his wardrobe—a silk shirt and slacks...very 90s, right?—and stormed away, telling me he was going to look for a bar. I wasn't really nervous. Nobody here really had that rapist vibe. They all seemed like silly girls to me, but hey, as long as someone was getting it on, I was fairly excited to see the show.

But then, our night took a bizarre, and yet fascinating turn. I gradually noticed that all the men around me were disappearing. Mike was the first to wander off, and within five minutes, all the other dudes had left. I looked around me and saw mostly women, and a strange mix of women, of all ages: teenage stoners, big-breast MILFs, big-nosed housewives, and a few librarians in the house.

I must admit: noticing an all-female cast did make me nervous and so I went to grab my black sweater, so I could cover my chill.

"So...what is happening?" I asked one of the regulars, an older woman, still beautiful, who replied with a snicker.

"What? What is so funny?"

She ignored my question and laughed again.

I was starting to become pissed and sat back down, folding my arms and sulking a bit. However, the joke was on me. Everyone was waiting for something. And that spaced, cackling laughter was not really avoidance but more like a "You have to see it to believe it" sort of warning.

I felt slightly nervous as I heard trumpets playing in the background.

All of the women in the room quickly stood up in respect.

"What's going on?" I asked to silence.

Strange, binaural music started to play in the background and I instantly fell into a weird, almost ethereal state of mind, with plenty of butterflies flapping around in my stomach.

I had a bad feeling about this. The lack of male presence here informed me that the party was just about to "begin." I looked around nervously, anxious to make my exit, if I only knew where the exit door was located and where Mark went.

Just then, the big doors to the right flung open. There stood a handsome, muscular man with a devious smile and very malevolent eyes.

"I am the Roman Emperor," he said with a smirk, proudly showing off his bare chest and chiseled abs. He wore black boxers and a mock little Caesar crown to emphasize the point.

He really did have the eyes and the brows of a mad Roman Emperor. But I have to admit he had a wild animal magnetism about him. Whenever he spoke, his charisma burned through us all. His body was buff and we all probably wondered just how big he was down there.

But I think it was his entitlement "role" he played that really made the women in the room shudder with erotic anticipation.

The Emperor walked around the room, surveying his subjects. "Line up immediately. No, in a square." He instructed the women to make a three-pronged line, a perfect square of female subjects, here to appease the Roman deity.

"In case you're new here," he said to various women in the crowd, most of whom he didn't recognize, "this is how we play Roman Emperor. When you are in this room, I own you all. One word and your head comes off. I could send you to the lions right now for treason!"

I kept thinking, Was this for real?

It seemed so over the top, and yet I was far too horrified to make a scene. I worried that if I did speak up, the "Emperor" was sure to choose me and do God knows what. I could have tried to make a run for it, but I wasn't even sure how to get out of this place, much less find my absent husband.

I had no idea what to do, so as the Emperor began pacing around the square, looking at his various subjects, I just tried to shrink back and remain incognito as much as possible.

The Emperor first noticed a young redheaded girl towards the front of the row, probably 20 years of age. She stared straight ahead, afraid to meet his glaring eyes.

Whether he was delusional, a method actor, or an experienced pervert, the fellow sure got into his role. He hardly ever spoke a word. He simply took what he wanted from whoever tickled his fancy. As soon as he sensed fear in the girl's face, he began paying closer attention to her, grazing her face and neck with his hands.

He sniffed her a few times and let the scent of her perfume overtake his senses. He responded by breathing closer to her neck, caressing her nape with his soft lips. The girl sighed, blushingly aroused.

"Are you a good girl?" he whispered into her ear.

"Yes," she said firmly, closing her eyes as he reached his arm across her chest. He took his time unbuttoning her rosy patterned blouse. When he finished, he ordered her to take off her blouse and her black bra and show everyone in the room her breasts. The fact that everyone enjoyed the view at once really made the images vivid in my mind. I remember the shape of her areolas and the pinkish hue of her big nipples. I remember her exact face as the Emperor squeezed her nipples and mashed her tits around, demonstrating his power—one of respectful silence.

Just as I began to calm myself, figuring he chose her as his "sacrificial virgin," he caught us off guard. He walked over to the MILF in the room, a cute little blonde soccer mom in her early 40s who was already trembling in his presence. For some reason, all the women here were scared out of their minds, but never dared to object to the power of the Emperor. They all seemed to crave his touch. They wanted his attentive and jealous eyes, but they couldn't take the magnitude of his desire.

For a moment, I wondered if I could

take it. His brutality. His Emperor-sized lust. It would be a challenge and I love a good challenge.

As I thought it over and tried to hide in the background, I caught sight of the Emperor already opening up that MILF's skirt. The mommy gasped as he lustfully undressed her, lifting her skirt and pulling her granny panties down to the floor. He looked over her blonde bush and admired her camel toe. I could see her breathing rate accelerating as he knelt down to her pussy and put his lips to her neatly shaved mound. She looked down at him in surrendering excitement. If he fucked her now, all she could do is cum in objection.

But then, another group sighed, as he abandoned the naked MILF and again started to survey the room. I felt the dread building as he worked his way over close to me, taking time to touch breasts and beavers along the way.

I tried so hard to avoid his eyes, to not look the least bit interested or willing. However, my reluctance to play his game only provoked him.

He came up to me and stared deeply into my eyes, not allowing me to ignore him. I snorted at him in contempt as he looked down at my breasts, hidden behind my now buttoned jacket.

"You don't belong here."

How did he know? I wondered.

I said nothing, not wanting to play his game.

He began smiling me down, as if he already knew the outcome of the night. "I know who you are. Meryl."

My eyes shot wide open! How did he know me? I tried to ignore the comment, but couldn't hide my sudden chill traveling down my spine. He saw me gulp in terror. He knew he was getting to me. And what the hell, all I could think about was letting him fuck me just to get this charade over with. Why does he have such unexplained sexual charisma? Why do women fear him and yet want him? Who is he really?

He started slow and spooned me from behind, slowly dancing his way into a more intimate position. He put his hands on my tummy, sensing my initial objection to intimate touching. I know exactly what he's thinking. He's thinking if he keeps touching me and slow simmering me like this, I'm going to let him touch me in other ways. He's right. And I don't know why.

"Who are you?" I whispered to him, very aware of his heated breath all over my neck.

"You know who I am. We've chatted before."

The Internet guy? I asked myself. I flinched, pretending to be oblivious, but somehow he seemed to know everything I was thinking. I couldn't hide myself from him. So why deny him any private details of my body?

My irrational mind was getting nutty by this point and I was trying so hard not to let him fuck me. I kept reminding myself of Mark and how this was probably not what he had in mind for spicing up our marriage!

The mysterious Emperor began kissing my neck, slowly letting me soak in his essence. I felt almost disgusted with myself when I felt my first pussy sting. He was turning me on. And it wasn't right. But I couldn't deny what was happening to my nerves—to my senses.

"Am I as sexy as you pictured me on the Internet?" he asked.

I fumed back as I crawled out of the spoon hold. "I don't know who you are! And I don't want you near me!"

I slapped him square in the face. As soon as I did, my chest was on fire. Sparks were flying all over my face and I was becoming soaking wet.

He knew this instinctively and grabbed me by force, putting me back in the spoon position. I gasped in reluctant pleasure.

"Mmm, no...," I could barely whisper as he shoved his hand into my dress and past my blue panties. "Oh God!" I shrieked, as the Emperor found my clit and rubbed it ever so softly, just the way my kitty requested. I whimpered back, feeling the throbbing and his steamy, minty breath all over my neck.

"Where is your husband, Meryl?"

"I don't know!" I yelled with a crack in my voice. "I-I'm not supposed to be here."

"I know. That's why I chose you."

He intensified his clit loving and got a great shot at it, since I was throbbing and showing that thick little switch all over the place. I was so close to cumming and he hadn't even started the show yet. As I looked around the room, helpless to resist, unwilling to object, I noticed all the other women watching me—in that same terrified but turned-on state of mind. They wanted to see him fuck me and live it by watching.

I felt the culmination building. He was just inches away from fucking me, and I still couldn't think of an excuse—or even a notion—on why I should make it stop. I was part of the show. They all came to see me orgasm.

No. I stopped myself from cumming and took his hand off me. I looked at him from the spoon position, halfway disgusted and halfway wanting to swallow his spunk.

Oh no. I think he read my mind.

He let go of the spoon hold and turned me forward, just so he could push me down to my knees. He made sure I got a perfect ringside seat of his ringer, as he pulled his boxers down, exposing his fucking huge 10-inch cock.

"Is this what you wanted to see, Meryl?"

I didn't know how to answer that. But I couldn't help but stare into his head, you know which one, as I looked into the eye of that great circumcised beast.

I was just two seconds away from gagging on that cock, just to entertain the audience, just to steal the scene. But I resisted. I walked away from him, barely suppressing my flooding pussy, barely able to stand the chaffing of my very hard nipples against my bra. Oh, how I wanted to tear that bra off right then and there.

He walked closer to me like a dog in heat, or more like a predator ready to pounce on his weakened prey. I didn't know how much longer I could resist. Almost instinctively, I took off my jacket and threw it to the floor. I was suddenly aware of how hot it was in the room and how sweaty my chest was becoming.

He walked up again and grabbed me in a powerful kiss. His lips invaded my privacy and my tongue went on the defensive, battling his tongue for power. This was not a good defense strategy though, as it only helped to make me hornier and to fuel his desire.

In one very smooth and animalistic gesture, he pulled down my blouse, exposing my bra to the excited girls. He put his hands through my bra and pressed on my hard nipples. His cock was so huge he didn't even have to carefully slide it in. It was already knocking on the door and ready to blow the house down.

I only had one argument left, and I spoke as clearly as I could while muffling through panting and moaning. "I shouldn't do this to Mark."

"Mark?" he laughed, taking one hand off my tit and securing my pelvis, holding onto my pubic mound for dear life. "Where do you think Mark is?"

"Where?"

"Well, let's put it this way. Either he's watching us...wanting you to get fucked...or he's being held hostage and the only way out of it is to let the Emperor fuck his beautiful wife. So what do you say?"

His hand massaging my mound and my pussy already growing wet enough to accommodate two of him, all I could do was to react by instinct.

I reached down and pulled my panties off, giving him the perfect angle to fuck me from behind.

"Ohhh, Jesus!" I screamed as his huge head entered me, squishing through the lips and soaking up all that feminine glory. The deeper he put that snake into me, the more pressure he put on my aching little G-spot. "Oh God!" I squealed again, as he increased the pressure and plowed my pussy with that fucking huge dong. He pounded my G-spot like a tyrant while fingering my clit with his other hand. The room was totally silent except for my screaming and the sound of the Emperor's balls slapping up against my ass. All the other women were watching. Some of them were playing with their nipples; some were masturbating. Some were just watching me, not flinching but taking in the experience.

"Your husband's watching, Meryl. I want you to cum all over my cock while he watches."

"Uhnn!" I screamed at his shocking talk, drenching his cock like he wanted and already starting my clitoral orgasm.

"Oh yes...cum on it."

"Ohhhh Mark! Ohhhh Mark! Make me cum!" I bellowed out, as I turned red in the face and rode his cock like a human vibrator. When he finally came in me, his spunk squirted for minutes on the end. One right after the other, as if the dude hadn't come in months...or maybe just had a whole fucking farm of semen down there, who knows.

The Emperor never said another word to me, nor did the women who flicked it to my orgasm.

Mark and I later met up at the bar. We

didn't say a word to each other either. I never asked Mark what his little game was, but I imagine it was something goooood since he didn't even ask me about my adventure, apparently feeling far guiltier than I did.

It's a shame, really. So many adventures, and yet so few stories to tell at parties.

4 A SECOND CHANCE FOR LOVE

Have you ever wondered what might have been? Dear, sweet Richard. Whenever I think of the song "Send in the Clowns," I think of us. Just a couple of fools with bad timing, making the same silly mistakes over and over again.

The first time you noticed me, my head was in the clouds. I was lost, cynical beyond my years, and desperately in love with another man. To be honest, I did notice you even back then. I noticed how despondent you looked every time we spoke small talk. I saw the aching in your eyes, your heart. I wondered if it was me. But then...I was really in no position to find out the truth. Was I?

And you were not the type to put your feelings out there. No one could ever read you, Richard. You bottled up your emotions so well, to the point that you almost became asexual to us—your friends, your admirers, the ones you always kept at an arm's length.

By now, you know the ego of a 19-year-old girl is not very subtle and curiosity is never enough to change her mind. Now, 14 years later, I stand before you a woman. A broken woman. And however, selfishly, I wonder what might have been.

Now, of course, I'm well grounded and you're in the clouds. The last time we met, or at least our eyes met, you wouldn't even look at me. Your face looked in my direction and you said hello in front of our mutual friends, but you didn't feel it—you fought against feeling something. I don't know if you wanted to hurt me or if you are truly just "over" me.

Maybe the site of your former dream girl, all grown up and worn out, disappoints you. The shoe is on the other foot. But I still entertain those fantasies. The silly, romantic, and blind ones that no one but I could believe. The grand drama of you, saying you've always been in love with me. That nothing I could ever do would disappoint you. That maybe, somewhere in that deep mind of yours, you have dreamt of the day when you could finally say your piece.

Well, Richard, that day happened. The

second week I was back in town, I know our eyes met and I noticed you looking at me. For our second encounter, you didn't look away, shunning me or silently judging me. This time, I saw you staring. You knew who I was. You were thinking something about me. That's what I want to know—the thought. What you really feel. What you have denied me and everybody for so many years.

I know I am bound to see you again, given our mutual friends, and our mutual love of coffee at the old bookstore on Raymond Street. Someday, maybe, hopefully, you will read this letter. Maybe holding me in your arms. Maybe laughing about the silliness of it all. Maybe even feeling a twinge of regret at the way things turned out and feeling a sudden urge to hug the lowly Amanda who never deserved you.

Richard, I was delighted to learn that you still remember my name. Somehow, you speaking my name did make me feel wanted and loved—not just as your long-time secret crush—but as a lifelong friend.

"Hello, Amanda," you said with that odd tone in your voice, that ambiguous, non-committal tone that makes you seem so mysterious to outsiders. You never actually said if you noticed me, or noticed how I got all dolled up for you, wearing a black dress and blue blouse with see-through sleeves and a shawl. I didn't just comb my hair for you, I styled it, making it curly the way I thought you liked it. Of course, that was only based on a vague inclination I had when we were teenagers...how you once remarked in church that you liked curly hair because it looks "Italian."

I may have Italian blood in my ancestry somewhere, but I'm a spoiled American white woman at heart, and my blonde locks are about my only redeeming feature. Of course, that never seemed to concern you before. You were always so altruistically interested in my mind, weren't you?

"That's a nice jeep," you remarked to me, eyeing my new white Land Rover.

"Heck yeah," I said, "It's a Land Rover. I'm a wild child."

You ignored me and said something predictably debonair. "I haven't had a chance to welcome you back to town. I've been so busy; I didn't really have a chance to hear what you had to say on the way out last time. If anything...er, did you have anything to say to me?"

"I have a lot more to say to you," I assured you, sassing it up, hoping to draw out your attention.

But once again, you fled.

You excused yourself from the store parking lot and I watched you walk back to your sports car, probably feeling on top of the world. No worries...it gave me a chance to size you up and check you out! You always did have a nice butt, my friend. Tight for sure...but you were never a flaunter. You kept all your best qualities tucked away.

Your brown hair, black slacks, and sexy Dolce and Gabbana glasses seems so much more attractive now that I'm a divorced, fully matured woman and you're no longer a boy, pushing 35 by my count. We allowed ourselves to grow up, didn't we? What's really funny though is that we sort of act the same way, even after all these years later. We both kept that childish giggle, that silly gullible nature. It was once such a cute thing, wasn't it? Our naiveté...before it landed me in an troubled marriage and you...well...not to judge, like I always do, but it landed you in a bit of a time capsule conundrum. Not to pry, of course, but I do wonder why you stayed single after all these years.

And why, even to this very day, you still hold something back from me. Well the joke's on you this time, buddy. Now, I have all the time in the world to figure out what's going on in your head.

Dearest Richard, I think I will long remember our latest conversation at the bookstore earlier today. How convenient it was that I found you there. Dare I suggest you were waiting for me? Or was I merely arriving there for you? All I know is that you made an old woman very happy today, humoring her with the joy of your company for a full half hour.

"You are not old," you playfully counseled me. "Because if you're old that means I'm old. And I'm not ready to pass into the next age demographic yet."

Every time you told a silly joke, I gave you a hands-on-belly laugh, the kind that used to tickle you pink when we were young. Now, as "responsible" and well-read intellectuals, do such banal thrills still do it for you? Is your motivation now to make a girl laugh or to force her to think?

I must admit, dear Richard, I felt so turned on today when I saw you speak in front of that writing group. Silly me, I thought you were at the bookstore just to see little old me. I should have known you were there for a book signing, the successful author, the major success story. I suppose it's selfish of me to only notice these wondrous things about you now—when everything is so obvious.

"Don't be silly," you reassured me after the signing. "I always have time for an old friend."

I hope you saw the way I smiled at you, that longing, that warm and inviting "come hug me" smile. And I hope I didn't come across as too needy. The very idea of you making time for me, taking off a busy hour in your life to entertain an "old friend" was making me smile from ear to ear.

The day was growing old and I knew, within a few minutes, you could very well disappear from my life again—this time very much against my wishes—because of book-signing duties. This episode could have lasted an hour, since you did love to chatter with your readers. Suddenly, my dear, I felt that strange THIS-IS-IT moment. The same rush of adrenaline you probably had the day before I ran off to marry Old Jerk Face. But however cruelly, I never gave you the chance to speak your mind, did I?

I guess that's why I did it. "It" being, of course, the biggest risk a woman ever takes—to tell a man how pathetic and how desperately she's fallen for him. It was a reckless move, and one that went against everything the dating books and advice columns ever told me about how to handle relationships. But then again, following the crowd is what landed me in a bad marriage to begin with. As you slipped away from my fingers with every passing moment, I figured I had nothing to lose.

"Richard…" I said, just seconds away from the official beginning of the book signing. The woman was already introducing you in the background of our private conversation.

"I just want to say...I'm sorry...that I never gave you a chance. I think I knew how you felt all those years ago. I just never let myself admit it."

You looked up at me with the strangest face. Not the "What is she talking about?" face, thank God, but the "I can't believe she's saying this" face, which did make me feel good.

"And yes, it does feel good to know that even at 33 years of age, I can still turn heads and get asked out by guys on motorcycles on the street. Even so, the only man who has my attention is you. I don't know if that means anything anymore. I don't even know why I'm saying all of this to you. But maybe I'm speaking for the both of us. Maybe I've reached that point in my life where I can't stand the idea of missed opportunities. Or buried feelings. Or forced smiles."

I like the "forced smiles" bit. Maybe my little speech appealed to your literary mind. Or maybe you just thought I was batshit crazy. But I must admit; I loved the idea of rocking your little writing world and sending you to a long, boring book signing obsessing about what just happened. I knew it for sure now...as we both traded confused glances in between autographed copies, I was definitely on your mind.

"It was my own fault. I never acted. Just look at me. Right at the downhill slope of my life and I'm still single."

I so enjoyed our dinner out later that evening, having just barely stolen you away from your VIP night.

"I'm sorry if I interrupted your book signing. I hope you weren't trying to score with a writing groupie or something and I ruined your night. I would feel terrible."

"Well, the night's not ruined yet!"

I stared at you for a moment, not really angry, just kind of wistful.

"I'm not a writing groupie, Richard. I'm not even much of a reader. But I knew you long before any of this happened. The real you."

You waited. Thinking things over and giving me a slight heart attack, waiting in dreadful expectation.

"I know, Amanda."

"Do you?"

"I know why you're here. And I know you're waiting for me to tell you off, or have some gigantic, dramatic moment where I lash out at you and then kiss you in fiery passion."

"Is that an idiom?"

"Um...no, that's just a cliché. The point is..."

Pause. Pause. Pause.

"...I never hated you. You don't owe me any apology. My feelings for you will never change. Regardless of whether we get together or just stay platonic...it doesn't really matter. We're friends. Maybe to some people 'friends' doesn't mean anything. But it does to me."

Dearest Richard, it only took us about 20 minutes or so to ruin our good friendship with impulsive sex. Our mutual attraction was so intense, I was pretty sure something was going to happen within the week. But on the same day? And in my jeep?

I loved the way we kissed. The look in your eyes was breathtaking and invited me over to your lips, ever so subtly, so gradually coming closer. Yes, I wanted you to make the first move, like you should have done years ago, like I crave for you to do today.

Your strong hands held me tight, but gently. It felt so nice to be treated gently again, to be adored, respected, and reawakened, after so many nights of violence and uncertainty. And when you kissed me, your lips smacked of sincerity. Of devotion. Maybe it wasn't all what I deserved, but it is what I wanted—and for the first time in my life, it was the thing I knew for sure that I wanted.

I whispered softly in your ear, "Come with me to the backseat."

I was so excited as you followed me back to the rear of the jeep. You awakened something deep in me and my flower bloomed for you. Every time you kissed me, it rained. Every time you touched the back of my neck, my garden became a tropical rainforest. I wanted you so much, dear Richard, to feel your strong, soft hands on my chest, to feel your warming lips sample my every crevice.

A woman always knows who she likes and she always dresses to impress. This time I dressed up for you, sweet lover, packaging my beauty and my natural artwork just for you, so that you could unwrap them and taste their sweetness. Taste me, Richard, taste my every orifice, my every freckle and mole. I want to bathe in your attention.

Being naked with you that night wasn't enough. Even when I took off my dress and exposed my camisole to you, a sight I could tell you much appreciated, it never satisfied me. I wanted to give you everything that night. To bare all my clothing and let you explore the fields and the valleys of my body.

I still remember my first one—you paid so much fond attention to my breasts, I couldn't help but quiver and moan as you sucked my intimacy away. The second one was unexpected—I really didn't expect you to water my garden, and to do it so well! Your tongue slipping in and out of my lips, caressing my humid bulb, I pulled you in close to me, desiring you not just in or on my skin but inside my creamy, warm center.

As we wrestled in the back of my jeep, late one night in an abandoned parking lot, I felt an amazing feeling of safety, love, and intensity. I think I did trust you already, but trust doesn't explain why I was suddenly naked with you and tasting your sugary goodness on the tip of my tongue.

No, I wanted you because I knew you were gentle and I knew, once again, that lovemaking itself could be gentle. When I climbed on to the backseat, I was so comforted that you took the time to position your frame carefully on mine and that you took so much concern to enter me carefully, exploring my depths with patience and with playfulness. When you filled my void with your unbreakable spirit, you reminded me of how beautiful life can be. Even in a world of regret, abuse, and mistrust, lovemaking prevails. Beautiful, gorgeous nude portraits of imperfect but sexy bodies and a comforting soundtrack of his and her singing in ecstasy.

Richard, I felt every moment of that next orgasm. Still going slow, you pushed and pulled with perfect rhythm predicting my every pulsating tremor.

You took me by the hand and guided

me to pleasure, rubbing myself away of haunting memories and embracing the calm and warmer waters of the now.

"Say my name," I whispered, holding my head and curling my hair, in the midst of my final and most powerful orgasm.

A sexy man's voice echoed my name as I felt the steady but peaceable vibrations. I remember so crisply our nude bodies sweating against each other, our nipples touching, and our lips on fire, tasting anything we could get our mouths on.

Dear Richard, I write this final letter as you lay next to me in bed, thoroughly exhausted from a hot date in which you scored with your ultimate groupie. I lay next to you and cuddle, careful to leave my bosom exposed for your wake-up time. I want you to remember me this way when your beautiful eyes flutter awake; naked, hiding nothing, and always your adoring lover.

Dear Richard, I can't wait for you to wake up so I can hear your wonderfully scenic vision, the one that describes not who I was, or who I long to be, but who I am.

Only you can reassure me. Only you can give me a second chance. You have always known the real me. So I will stifle my tongue and try my best to avoid suffocating you in lovey-dovey mush. I will simply look deep into your telling eyes and wait for you to tell the story.

5 SEXY ALIEN PRISON BREAKS

"Greetings ladies, germs, and my androgynous friends. My name is Qualleps. I believe my parental units named me either out of spite or laziness, since the name "Qualleps" sounds as if it is a name of great meaning...but it isn't. It is possible I was named because of a computer malfunction or perhaps an inferior form of artificial intelligence. I had no siblings. I did not procreate with females. I lived as a slave on a planet called Hirayknu, whose government officials beat and tormented slaves for their own sadistic pleasure."

"I am telling you this because I want you to understand that I have had a difficult life. And I am more than happy to take all of my rage, disappointment, and anger out on you. You are prisoners of this world. You didn't cross me, but you crossed somebody. And that is what landed you here. I don't presume to make judgments about you. I am merely doing the bidding of others, others who have paid me quite well to make sure you suffer."

"So it is in your best interests to serve me well. Do not question my authority. Do not cheat, steal, or lie. Serve your time honestly, get off my planet. Do what you want with your life from that point. Do we understand each other?"

"Yes, Lord!"

This is the statement I say aloud to every prisoner who inhabits QUC-5, my "holding planet." There is no established galactic term for this small planet, except to call it an independent "holding" prison, a neutral territory, and a subcontracting party that serves the interests of pirates, empire rebels, and of course, "royal murderers," of whom planetary kings do not want to sentence to death but need to eliminate in a hurry.

Most beings might think of my plight as a rather sad one, forced to put away innocents and apologists alike, their cries for help constantly ringing in my ears and their frailties on clear display. The showers in particular are quite damaging to the ego, if not the skin. Males, females, hermaphrodite, and gonochoric beings all forced to strip naked and wash themselves in genetically enhanced H20, with the occasional acid bath to the species that can handle the nice, relaxing burn.

I watch them all strip. Not only because it pleases me, but also because it is important to establish my power over the prisoners. They are morally confused and ruthless, and most that come here have little respect for anything. What they do respond to is aggression and protocol. If I overpower them, I retain control of this planet, this facility. If I break my stone-cold facade, and flinch for just a minute in a momentary lapse of compassion, I will lose control over everything.

What's great about my position as a space warden is the fact that I have total freedom over the rehabilitation process. The prisoners are sent here with a minimum time period served recommended by the slave traders and are subject to my own personal interpretation of rehabilitation.

Rehabilitation? I hardly believe in it. Most rebels who come in here for murder are victims, expatriates, and prisoners of war and can hardly fathom the concepts of "right" and "wrong," since they have been trained for survival and raised in a galaxy that knows only nomads and barbarians.

Few of them respect me initially. I am a

male humanoid of average height and gray skin. I have a muscular build...but you have to understand that only humanoids find masculinity sexually arousing. Some beings that come through these iron plutonium wrought doors find flexibility arousing, or perhaps the absence or the versatility of form, the more intriguing idea.

I am of the more simplistic variety of species. I admire humanoid qualities, but then again, I admire all the characteristics of all female species. While I am a fan of large mammary glands (and the more the better), I also have a weakness for shape shifters and naturally elongating beings.

This job definitely comes with its perks. As I am not affiliated with any government or religious order, I am enslaved to no concept of morality. In fact, my absent parental units avoided all discussions of morality in my youth, no doubt fearing the implications of order and precedent in a universe built on chaos and freedom. Nevertheless, I have managed to bring a sense of justice to this planet—a trader's morality.

The ultimate rule being that no one disrespects the rule of the traded. You always give something of equal value to the ones who trade with you. To cheat, lie, or imply is a cardinal sin. And everyone in my prison knows that dishonesty is going to get you double the prison sentence.

Yes, I am a stickler for reform and for respecting authority. Then again, having no moral guidance by society, you might say I'm a bit of a pushover...at least when it comes to sex.

Oh yes, the females of practically every species will negotiate with sex almost as soon as they figure out there is no possible way out of the prison or off the planet. Now the first time they suggest a sex-for-freedom contract, I ignore it. Because fifty percent of these females are bluffing, hoping to get some love and understanding just because they flutter their eyelashes or make their breasts dance.

But that's not negotiation. Losing prisoners, in addition to breaking contracts—stuff that could land me in a neutral court—costs me money in grants and awards. The more prisoners I keep, the more money I get from empires, pirates, rebels, and other entities who want to be assured that their "contributions" are still being indefinitely detained.

So in order for me to even consider releasing some sexy silver seductress and looking the other way while she buys transportation out of here, I have to get something of very high value in exchange for my help. My negotiation is firm. I want everything. No teasing. No making promises that you can't keep.

And it's not exploitation. It's called trading. But trust me, within forty-eight hours, they all get the point.

Ann the mystic mermaid is one of my favorites. She's not an actual mermaid but she's definitely a sea-dweller. She has gorgeous long, curly purple hair and eight rather bizarre looking squid legs. However, she knows how much humanoid men adore breasts, so she accentuates her huge breasts, wearing a homemade push-up bra she designed from her prison uniform. No, I'm not much of a stickler for wearing the same, boring black jumpsuits. I like variety...especially when that smoking, custom-designed dress is used to hike up her NN-cup breasts. Not a bit oversized, since she actually stands at over ten feet tall.

"Warden Qualleps, can we have a word with you?" she says during our lunch hour, folding her arms and nervously twirling her tentacles.

"What's that?" I say, playing cool, not even looking her in the face.

"We don't desire to stay here any longer," she says, alluding to some parasite that exists within her body or something like that. I didn't quite get that whole spiel. "Is there anything we can do to change your mind—perhaps, to let us out early for good behavior?"

I shrug it off. "I'm the warden. You're the prisoner. You have no money. What could you possibly offer me that would make me think about turning you loose?"

"Well," she smiles wickedly, "Perhaps there is some other arrangement we can come to...we are willing to do...anything to influence your decision."

I look her in the eye and then check out those massive breasts and greedy little tentacles that are already trying to grab me. She smiles, enjoying the fact that I'm fantasizing about her, just wondering what kind of scary things she could do to me with such flexible tools.

"Aaaarrrr!" I scream while fucking her huge tits in a private shower room.

"Oh yes...we like...we like..."

I ignore her weird mannerisms and focus on those huge naked mounds of flesh bouncing around my cock like an avalanche. My 10-inch penis is hardly big enough for those massive orbs with violet-colored, glowing areolas.

"Oh yes...hold them together," I command. She uses her tentacles to tighten her breasts together, squeezing the life out of my cock.

The first thing people ought to know

about fucking mermaid or sea-dwelling beings is that they never lay down for anyone. They prefer fucking while they are floating in the air, defying gravity. They have the ability to become weightless and to take lovers along for the ride. And yes, experiencing a weightless titty fuck is nothing like the humanoid stationary version.

Just when I think I'm ready to cum, Ann the mystic mermaid puts one over on me. She senses my heavy breathing and contracting penis and then does what any tentacle monster would do—she stuffs one of those slimy things straight up my asshole.

"Ohhhh God!" I scream in embarrassed ecstasy. She nails the prostate gland perfectly and makes sure I ejaculate all over her wiggling tits with a vengeance. I watch helplessly as my ejaculate floats off her tits and drifts around in midair.

I inhale and exhale deeply, trying to catch my breath. She replies by laughing a vile little laugh, the type I imagine a tentacle-wielding serial killer might have.

It's always weird when you do it with legless beings...I'm actually kind of relieved she didn't ask me to fuck her in her squid parts.

I will keep my end of the bargain and let her out tomorrow night. She assures me she will arrange for her own transportation. I will never see her again. But that's the kind of fugitive alien sex one remembers forever.

My next negotiator is particularly nasty and makes it a point to challenge my authority in front of everyone. It's not surprising in the least, considering where Shu X comes from. She is from EvoCitrius, a planet in the Gamul Galaxy, one notorious because it's female-ruled. Men are the inferiors of her territory, so she resents every moment of being here, locked away by a male humanoid, of all the lowest creatures.

I do wonder who she had to double cross to be sent here—the last place in the universe, a time when you really look around you and realize you are alone in the universe. I feel bad for Shu X. Even though she is as hostile as they come, I can see she is very uncomfortable being jailed with males. But my guards ensure that no funny business occurs between the prisoners while in my custody. Besides, comfort and propriety is not really a major factor in a prison planet in the middle of nowhere.

That's not to say that Shu X isn't a treat to behold. She is what one might call a "preferred taste." She is humanoid in form, but had blood-red hair that seems to just flow out of her head. Her eyes are crystalline and her three breasts were magnificent in form.

But what I will remember most about Shu X is her very unique flirting style.

"You are a disgusting being," she hisses at me, after requesting to meet me alone in my office.

"Why is that? You're the one locked up in here. Maybe you're the one whose actions were disgusting."

"You Cauraduan slug! You vile slime!"

"Is this your way of sweet talking me? Because it's not working."

She squints her devilish eyes and glows at me with radiating light. She grabs me by the neck to make sure I understand the negotiation.

"I could crush you like a worm right now, male," she says in fury. "But I understand you to be a peaceful trader. Therefore, I am prepared to offer you something in return for my unconditional release."

"Oh yeah? Why should I?"

She roars, "Or else you will have a bloodbath to contend with!"

Her fuming answer is one of desperation. She probably realizes she is powerless without her weapons and without her home planet's support. But to let her keep her pride, I pretend as if she's a real threat. And I pretend as if this isn't a pity fuck.

"What do you offer, female?"

She looks deep into my eyes, her slits barely human and a bit ghostly. "I will allow you to conquer my sex."

I raise my brow.

She gets right into my face and grits her teeth. "But you're not going to enjoy it."

"Want to wager on that?"

"Aaaahhhh!" Shu X screams like a warrior queen, as she inserts my stone hard penis into her super tight sexhole. Shu X's species only has one existing orifice, and it combines the best pleasures of oral, vaginal, and anal penetration that other species have taught us. Her sexhole is more like a vacuum than a canal, and as hard as I fuck her is as hard as she sucks me in deeper.

"Mmmmm!" I cry out with a tightened, red face.

"Stab harder, weakling!" she demands, taking a warrior's perspective of procreation. On her planet, inadequate males are practically sent to death camps. The only males who survive are sex slaves, capable of superhuman stamina. Fortunately, for me, I'm not fucking her to impress her.

I tense my muscles and focus on controlling my breathing, even though that vacuum hole is sucking me in with a vengeance. I can't help but admire Shu X's great body as she rides me vigorously on my desk. Her red bush bounces up and down as she intensifies the speed, determined to make me cum early so that she can feel like the winner. Her fiery pink nipples across her huge chest are beautiful to behold, even as three supple breasts slap against my face.

"Yesss..." she gloats, as she feels my imminent orgasm coming on. "Show me what a weak man you are!"

"Aaahhh!!" I howl out, feeling both intense pain and pleasure, as she locks down my penis inside of her and throttles it into oblivion. She fucks and sucks me so hard, I can't even see her moving anymore. She's flashing around my vision as if fucking me at the speed of light.

As I ejaculate, the vacuum intensifies, greedily sucking up all that spermatozoid, which she will probably store inside of her and take it home for lab testing.

My shot was so volatile, it has left me dehydrated, out of breath, and completely devoid of all energy and motivation.

As I watch her get up, get dressed, and call for a ship, I realize...I'm so spent I couldn't even stop her from leaving if I tried. I have to admire a species that loses with such power.

The next negotiator, Amieliac, is quite a specimen. She's dressed in royal clothes and for some reason, as part of her prison sentence from Lustrus-5, she's required to stay in her clothes. They do make for strange-looking attire. She wears a sparkling red robe with huge hair and with what appears to be blue skin. It's nearly impossible to tell what kind of body she has under that queenly robe or how in the world she ended up here, when she probably belongs near an emperor's throne. She is young, probably just barely legal age on her home planet and with a princess's gaze.

But I don't ask questions. All I can do is negotiate.

She is already pushing me and asking for too much.

"I want to take a friend with me."

"That's not fair. Your friend has a different record, a different purpose here."

"This is nonnegotiable. She must accompany me. I must be let out of this place immediately."

"I can't do that..."

She looks at me coyly. "I have heard otherwise. That you grant...favors to your prisoners in exchange for services."

"I can't let two females out on the same day, okay? That's two for the price of one. It's not fair to me or my system here."

She thinks it over a moment and looks

at me in inviting compromise. "What if she were to join us? Then it wouldn't be two for the price of one. It would be an...even trade."

I look on, curious as can be, but trying not to give her too much credit.

"Is she all right with this arrangement?"

"I believe I can persuade her to be very generous."

"Ohhhh yes...so very generous," I gasp, as I find myself in a sexy alien sandwich atop my own personal bed. Amieliac's new friend Kra-Rose is going to work on my cock clutching that head tightly and slipping it into her petite mouth. Kra-Rose is indeed beautiful, with a face full of green innocence and white flowing hair. She stays on her knees and sucks it tenderly only making eye contact with Amieliac.

Amieliac, meanwhile, is forever prideful. She insists that my ultimate pleasure would be in making her cum, since her species is well known for their subtle, very rich genital flavors. So she sits on my face and makes me lick her up good. Just as I suspected, she has a lean body, probably from hours a day working out in a palace.

I get the perfect view of this princess to be (probably just one rebellion away from usurping a throne). She straddles my head and plays with her small breasts, even as her pussy flows into my mouth.

Her taste is divine, like velvet sugar, or sunlight mixed with cinnamon. Just as I think life can't possibly get any better than this, Amieliac leaves behind her distinctive queenly mark. She contracts and quivers all over my face, her cumming pussy squirting me with yummy fruits and heavenly spices. Just as she comes, so too do I fill Kra-Rose's mouth with my less than divine-tasting spunk. Whatever species she is, she gives amazing head—her mouth feels like a warm fountain, like hot springs on a male's hot cock.

We all get dressed, and I wait patiently as the two females finalize their ride home.

"Good journey," I say in respect.

Amieliac looks at me in judgment. "I will remember you, Qualleps. I remember everyone's good deeds. And I also remember the people who insist on 'trading.' When I am queen again, I will come looking for you."

Amieliac and her friend—still gagging me out of her mouth—send me a chilly look of indifference before leaving the room. That sounds like trouble.

Oh well. What can you do...Over 500 alien bribes a year, you're bound to piss off one queen.

I won't fret about it. Whatever rebellion she's talking about is probably lifetimes from now. In the meantime, I have a whole new batch of prisoners coming in tomorrow. I never break the rules or exploit the innocent. I just happen to be very easy to persuade when it comes to a pretty face.

6 THE GREATEST TEST OF A MAN'S LOVE

For thousands of years, human beings have rationalized on why they do bad things. They have blamed religion, politics, and racial hatred, anything as a scapegoat. We use anything to distract us from the notion that we are what we are. We, the human race, do very bad things. It's in our nature.

And every time I have to listen to some ancient professor yack on about the constitution, the bible, or any other ancient relic that surmises to dictate "morality," I just want to shoot myself in the face. I think someday I will look back on my college days—a lifestyle that most people consider irrational, dangerous, and chaotic—as the one point in my life that really made the most sense.

Everywhere I turn, all I see are people laughing, taking drugs, having sex, and criticizing everything under the sun as "ignorance."

I walk to school from down the street, minding my own business and trying to look as casual as possible. Just another doomsday white girl in Florida, living in a dorm and dressing down, wearing a maroon cardigan, a striped blouse and light orange jeans. I am a brunette and thus never have all the fun, nor do I have the fighting Irish thing. I'm just a girl, with nothing much to say. Hey, I didn't try to be fashionable, nor did I ask for any attention.

But that does stop guys from trying?

Local player "Jake" speeds up his walking pace just so he can stop and walk me to school.

"Hey, Lisa. Long time no see."

"Oh yeah, we are such great friends, aren't we?" I send him a dopey look.

"We are good friends. But sometimes I think we're both too sexy for our own good."

I looked Jake up and down. He was sort of attractive. A jock look to be sure, buffed up, and always flaunting that hard body with tight jeans and a short-sleeved white shirt that showed off his biceps. Personally, I never understood the whole appeal about muscular guys. They still looked like gorillas to me.

"So you want to go out and get some coffee later?" He said, trying for the umpteenth time.

"No, I don't."

"Man, you're so defensive!" he said, reflecting back that rejection and wiggling his face in confidence. "Why have you become so jaded? What asshole broke your heart to make you this cruel?"

"Why is it cruel to say that I don't want coffee with you?"

"Are you afraid that you can't control yourself around me? You'll lose yourself..."

"No... more like I just don't care. I see no redeeming qualities in you."

Jake backed off and laughed, impressed at my high bitch level and trying to figure out the secret motivation as to why I was so mean.

"There is no real secret, Jake. I just don't think you're the type of guy I'm looking for..."

"Oh, you have a type, huh?" he says, side profiling, doing that alpha-male face they all do so well. "Look, I'm not asking to fall in love. Maybe you're not my type at all, you ever thought about that? Maybe I'm just trying to be nice and friendly and you're treating me like shit for no good reason. And you know what? Maybe you're crying inside too."

I stared him down. There was nothing else to really say but...

"Oh yeah, fuck it Jake! Fuck it just like that!"

After school, I spent the rest of the afternoon letting Jake fuck me, reaching for that G-spot he was so sure existed. I never actually felt it, but just the feeling of his cock slamming against me was more than enough to make me come.

More importantly, letting him fuck me shut him up really good. It's amazing how little a guy has to say to you after he sees you naked and blows his wad in a condom. I wasn't thrilled with the way Jake's heavy body attacked me missionary style for nearly a half-hour, but it sure did beat his lame coffee suggestion.

Jake began tensing up and talking like a red-faced drill sergeant. He spiked that condom good, but made one big mistake.

"Don't touch my hair," I warned him, as he took his damned hands off my head.

"Aaaahhh!" he said, coming deeply like a porn star. I must admit to being much quieter. Maybe volume is all about who wants it the most.

"So what now?" Jake asked me, figuring we were supposed to have some big emotional talk. His silence was so beautiful, during the short time that it lasted. He leaned over in bed and insisted upon having deep, meaningful eye contact. "Now...I think you ought to leave. Because you smell weird and I don't want you to taint my bed. It smells like perfect lavender."

He laughed merrily as he got dressed, thankfully leaving my super-clean bed behind. He couldn't help but show off his abs and his moderately sized, flaccid dick, as he dressed himself, so anxious to impress me with his greatest assets.

"Thanks for letting me see it one last time," I said with a smirk.

"No prob. Call me sometime."

"Don't have a phone."

"My cock needs no appointment."

That one almost made me laugh, but I never give guys the satisfaction of seeing a real smile. I tend to like sex better without love. It's so much more interesting to see what they do, when they can tell you're not really that attracted to them.

Take Matthias, for example. I like to call him Drama King because he is a self-professed poet and "blogger" who "tells it like it is." Of course, he has a Facebook page with only 30 or so people from school, but who are we to humble his huge ego?

This guy is another one of "those" who can't stop talking to me or about me.

Every time I open my SMS, he texts me, asking me deep questions and making all sorts of weird texting jokes that he probably found from a book. What I find most annoying is the fact that he always has to start his texts with...

"You know what I just realized...?" or...

"So...you know what I was thinking...?" or...

"Guess what?"

I get the whole trying to whet my appetite thing, but honestly, it's really annoying to answer a text just to read a rhetorical question.

Matthias, the cinnamon-skinned poet, showed up outside of my job at the fast food restaurant, in typically dramatic fashion, holding a bouquet of flowers and dressed in a blazer and a sports jacket. He either loved me or just loved causing a scene.

I went out to meet him staring at the flowers and looking slightly like death, dressed in an embarrassing orange corporation shirt, a gigantic apron, and very short black shorts. I remembered thinking, if this was a marriage proposal, this would be the all-time worst.

"Hello Matt," I said as politely as possible.

"Hello, Lisa. My heart yearns for you. Your beauty shines even now, in the midst of this ordinary scene."

"Okay," I shrugged.

"Your loveliness is timeless. Why, just yesterday I wrote five poems inspired by you."

I puffed out my cheeks, sort of impressed that he was this obsessive about me, dressed only in my work clothes and sans makeup. "Well...thank you for the flowers," I said as I took them from his hands, wondering if my boss would mind if they went into the business dumpster or if he would consider these "personal garbage."

"The flowers are only metaphorical. You are the true beauty."

I noticed a few of my co-workers giggling inside the building, probably thinking what a lucky girl I was. If only it felt like something real...

"I can only humbly request your presence for a grandly romantic day, this Saturday. It would be my privilege to have you attend."

"I don't think...I want to do that," I said, grimacing slightly, wondering if he'd cry or maybe start yelling Shakespeare.

"Oh...I see."

"Yeah. Just not my thing."

"Ah." He stood still, watching me, waiting for me to say something savage. But truthfully, I didn't really have anything mean to say. I just said what I was thinking.

"So...is there...anything else you want?"

"Oh, Matt! Come in me! Come in me!"

We skipped the grand romantic date and instead I rode Matt's swelling dick in his studio apartment, which looked like a disco yoga dungeon to me.

"Look at me," he said, grabbing my cheeks and looking deep into my eyes. "Look at me when you come."

I rode him harder and kept close eye contact, never flinching.

"Oh Matt! I'm coming..."

"Me too!"

We came together and mixed fluids all the while staring into each other's eyes. I never quite felt the Tantric soul thing Matthias was talking about, but I have to give him credit for a very dramatic encounter. We fucked bare-ass naked on the carpet, surrounded by candles and incense. His body was only slightly doughy, but with the boyish outlines of muscles.

It was so nice to hear Matthias shut up for once. He remained silent for minutes on end, spacing out, lost in his own Chi.

"Well...", I said as I looked up at the starry wallpaper and the lava lamps, and every other strange item he felt compelled to use in home decoration.

"I better go now."

I never say the right thing, of this I am aware. And it was hell to contend with both of these needy guys during the next week. Jake acted all macho about it, while Matthias artfully approached the subject. In their own distinctive ways, they each communicated the same thing. They both wanted me. They could say it in a million different ways, but it was the same basic thought. They were smitten.

Meanwhile, I was still confused by what exactly the two hunters wanted from me. I thought guys usually packed up and left after the first score, but these two rhinos seemed to gravitate toward me wherever I went.

Then—since all bad things happen for a reason—the relationship drama intensified, and I was left in a very awkward position.

"Who is he?" Jake barked, his bulging muscles out and ready to defend his woman's honor. "Is it that guy? That Internet stalker?"

"Yes, I guess that's him."

"That's bullshit. Matthias is a freak of nature. You think he digs you? That guy is just amazed that any woman would talk to him for longer than two seconds."

Jake folded his arms and scowled. "But I guess I'm the sucker, right? I'm the one that gets hurt. I wear my heart on my sleeve and I get burned. But it's all right, I see how it is."

I rolled my eyes as I tried to assure Jake that our time together wasn't just a fling. That I really felt something—whatever "something" means. But nothing I said seemed to calm him down. He was seeing red and wanted to take his anger out on Matthias. Meanwhile, the Drama King lived for this kind of thing, and he couldn't help but egg on his competition, hoping all of this drama would keep my attention. I suppose it did...like an episode of Twin Peaks. Like, I sort of want to see how it ends even though I don't get any of it?

"I am calling you out, Jake!" Matthias blasted over a megaphone, stepping all over the lawn outside Jake's apartment. "You are a peon. An inferior creature. And the woman I love has rejected you. Prepare to surrender, dear knight. Or I will unleash my wrath upon you!"

A crowd of bored college kids actually gathered around Matt hoping to see a very dramatic fight. Jake did soon wake up and got into a yelling and shoving match with Matthias, much to the excitement of the crowd. Police officers later came and broke everything up.

I suppose I felt responsible for all of this chaos in a way, though I think it's not really fair that men get to have all sorts of reckless sex and everyone looks the other way, but as soon as a woman does it, it becomes a major "issue."

The competition was on, and now both guys—their egos bruised and their dicks feeling threatened—were trying to outdo each other. First, they tried to top each other with presents: Matt bought me an expensive painting while Jake bought me an iPhone. Then, they tried to one up each other with commitment. Jake offered to move in with me, while Matthias took me to meet his mom and dad.

The whole thing was just getting ridiculous.

I ditched two more dates with both testy guys so I could enjoy some alone time. Maybe even have a night of introspection...and attempt to figure out where I went wrong and what I really want out of life. Maybe that's the mature way to handle it.

After a night of thinking things through, I decided the only mature thing to do was to have a long talk with them both and break the news gently.

So we arranged to meet in my grandmother's vacation house and have a few drinks. Matthias wore his preppy-style clothes, while Jake wore his usual muscle headgear. I tried to dress non-committed in every way, so I wore black pants and a white shirt, as if I just came back from work.

I told them I wanted to square away all the hostility and stay friends with everyone, no matter the decision I came to. They both reluctantly agreed, but couldn't resist smacking each other one last time.

"Well, if you choose Matthias, I hope you can break him away from the Internet and away from those pedophile chat rooms. And I hope you'll be happy together, you know, in therapy."

"Well, Jake, if the lovely Lisa chooses you, I hope your retarded children turn out happy...and get the same opportunities in life as normal kids."

"Okay, okay!"

I nervously began my speech standing in front of my captive audience who were leaning back on the couch. "I want you both to know that you're both...um...nice? And I find you both...attractive, in a way."

They waited impatiently while I thought my speech over.

"And I guess what I want to say is...I think life is very confusing. And lots of shit happens for no apparent reason. And that doesn't mean that, like, everything has to go according to plan. There is no predestination. We are everything and everyone."

Both guys look confused. All right, I pretty much epic-failed the big speech.

Suddenly, Matthias stood up from the

couch and walked over toward me. He didn't bother looking at Jake but spoke in his direction. "This is not the time for speeches. True romance calls for action. And so I take action just like the lovely Lisa deserves."

Matthias grabbed me in a passionate kiss. His lust was so intense I lost myself and started making little grunting noises. I didn't tell him to stop. I let him touch my face and put his hands through my hair. It would appear as if I made my choice.

Jake pouted, quite appalled at the way I unveiled my announcement. Of course, I didn't actually choose Matthias—he made one really big play that I had yet to recover from. Jocular Jake jumped up, figuring this was his cue to exit.

I peacefully broke Matt's kiss and looked at Jake, not wanting to see him leave.

As he stood silent, trying to figure out my mind, I felt Matt's fire and let him French-kiss me. I sighed heavily and began taking off his jacket, longing to see his naked body again.

The jock watched in confusion and unrest as Matthias unbuttoned my shirt, keeping me busy with a long, sweltering kiss. All the while he loved me, I continued to stare at Jake, silently communicating a thought that I didn't want to decide right then and there. Rather, I wanted to feel something. I wanted the night to go on.

Jake slowly approached us, forming an idea in his head, but unsure of the etiquette. He walked up behind me and kneeled to the ground putting his face on my ass and nibbling my cheeks through the pants.

Matt stopped kissing me and looked at me in surprise. I smiled at him, silently communicating a thought—prove yourself. He listened to my eyes and kissed me again, allowing Jake to sample me from behind, slowly pulling my pants down as Matt unbuttoned my shirt.

We said nothing but I was surprisingly vocal. I sighed and whined as Jake pulled off my pants and kissed my ass, gently tugging at my pink panties. I kissed my other lover in deep passion, letting him swoop off my blouse, exposing my matching pink bra.

I unhooked it from my back, letting it fall to the ground and giving both guys the chance to check out my big breasts. The same ones they suckled on just days ago...and the same ones they might get to enjoy again... if they learn to share.

Matt ravaged my breasts as soon as he saw my perky nipples. He was a bit of a tit hog, as he moved me over to the couch, lying me down, just so he could kneel and suck on both of my nipples.

I looked at Jake who seemed to be asking me what to do with his eyes. For a moment, I made him wait and watch Matt suck on my tits, just to make him a little jealous. Then, I opened my legs to him, showing him by pink panties that were getting wet in a hurry.

The jock made his way over to the other side of me on the couch and put his mouth to my mound, sniffing in my intimate scent. He pulled my panties off and I moaned softly, enjoying the sensation of my nipples being played with, while I felt a nice draft on my shaved pussy.

The muscle man put his tongue on my clit and I moaned aloud even before he began licking it. The sound of my moan only provoked Matt who began squeezing my nipples.

"Oh yeah!" I cried, my erogenous zones spinning. I looked at Matt, huffing and puffing, and swallowing my passion. "Kiss me..."

He kissed me hard and fast while Number Two licked my clit faster.

"Ahh!" I sighed, breaking the kiss and feeling the imminence of orgasm. I stood up on the couch, giving an eye signal to Matt to pull off his pants and sit his cock up nice and firm for me. I watched him do it...he pulled out his hard member for a moment, just letting me watch it. There it was, a perfectly hard stiffy standing there at attention and just begging for me to ride it. I slid it into my cunt, straddling him in front and leaving my back to Jake to do his worst.

Jake pulled his jeans down in one fast motion, exposing his cock and his balls—but only for the benefit of Matthias, who responded to the spiteful competition by fucking me faster and harder.

Jake squatted on the other side of me getting the perfect angle of my ass. I love the fact that Jake didn't even ask. He presumed. And that's what made it so fucking hot. He pushed that cock into my ass and fucked me right along with my boyfriend. Two cocks inside of me, scissoring my pussy and asshole...I was gushing all over the place and was just moments away from coming—and coming loudly for a change.

My two "devoted" lovers didn't even look into my eyes when they fucked me. They looked at my naked ass, my bare breasts, my pussy, and my stretched asshole.

And they looked at each other. They were so obsessive about this game; they started to take their aggression out on me. They fucked me rough and hard, just to see which one of them could make me scream the loudest. I don't think there was an official winner...but I came so hard I almost blacked out.

The night ended perfectly—with me in a small pool of cum.

Why did I screw up two perfectly good relationships with a meaningless ménage a trois and an out-of-nowhere double penetration? (Oh yes...believe me, both guys are completely weirded out now and won't even talk to me.)

I guess because I'm human.

And we all do very bad things...just because we can.

7 THE FIRST LOVE SPELL I CAST

Sarah Collins. She was the flame, the little fiery wick that ignited my soul and inspired me to do great things. She was also the little girl I lost, and the one true love I was deprived. When I first fell in love with her, I was but a boy, a slightly younger boy than I am now, now pushing 27. At one time though, I was a starry-eyed nineteen-year-old that worshiped the ground she walked on.

I remember as a boy gazing at her in church and instantly becoming drawn to her dark black hair and emerald green dress. She was meant for me, and I had the extended diary to prove my great eternal love for her.

Yet, to my chagrin, the next time I saw her, she was walking with him, the usurper and the chubby little man who stole my destiny from me.

The long walk back to the house was excruciating that night. No words would comfort me. I took no solace in the lovelorn poetry of old fools or in the alcoholic beverages of the night. Misery had overtaken me. Suffering won. I stood a defeated boy, far too slowly to make a play for her so late in the game.

He, the usurper, probably had the world to offer Sarah.

I, on the other hand, had not but one deck of cards.

When I first learned sleight of hand tricks involving cards, I was only thirteen. But I continued to study the craft and do the math in my head, so that I could easily impress small crowds and say something debonair like—

"And sir, I believe is this your card."

Oohs and aahs from the spectators. Yes, magic was quite the comfort hobby. And when I lost Sarah for the first and final time, I retreated into my magic. I moved well beyond card tricks. I craved the dark, black magic that was forbidden: darkness, villainy, and deceit...it all seemed to perfectly represent what was happening in my blackened heart.

Of course, most of my friends and companions dismissed my art, my talents, suggesting that I was merely using optical illusions to grow roses, disappear at will, and even summon ectoplasm out of thin air.

"There's no such thing as magic, Henry," my own father told me, discouraging me from sharing any news about my magic career. I even held a séance for my most cynical of followers...but they were too busy cracking jokes and getting wasted to notice that I had actually started contact with my great-great-great grandmother Mildred.

As I stubbornly clung to practicing magic and amateur sorcery, the world around me was changing. Sarah's new husband was making huge money in the stock market. Meanwhile, I was having trouble booking even a few shows a year, since my detailed descriptions of black magic performance seemed to alienate most of the family crowds.

But it was fitting. The black arts magician is always miserable, scowling, and unhappy. Maybe it's the deep, dark secret of the universe...what we want most alludes us. The negativity we spread surrounds us.

The first fire spell I cast was very appropriate and burned away the image of a familiar face. "I wish you happiness, without jealousy, and without an evil eye. I wish you love and peace. Goodbye."

I waved my staff and chanted a prayer.

The photo of her adorable, smiling face caught fire. Every time she smiled, she had a special look of tenderness, hiding her teeth but grinning fully with her eyes. And then she burned, and burned, and slowly, hopefully, was scorched from my memory.

Serendipity's bastard cousin is Irony. And he is a cruel bastard for sure. It was not but two weeks removed from the fire spell that a most unusual visitor graced me with her presence. I was attending a public arts show with family but became socially exhausted by the time early afternoon rolled around. I sought a quiet sitting place, away from the festivities, and far, far away from Sarah and her new husband, who insisted on tormenting me with their sudden and inexplicable interest in art.

However, despite my sincere attempts to be reclusive, and despite wearing my villainous cloak of darkness as a warning, one person still managed to find me.

Vicki Collins, Sarah's mother, approached me in mid-brood and sat herself next to me. She was probably late 30s at the time and is probably mid 40s by today. I don't recall what she was wearing that day but I do remember seeing that tender, no teeth smile with the grinning eyes that so impressed me about Sarah.

"It's been so long since I've seen you, Henry," Vicki said.

"Yeah, same here. How have you been?"

"Pretty good."

"We missed you at Sarah's graduation party."

"Ah, well, I didn't have a car. Didn't really have a way to get there."

"Oh, you should have told us. We could have picked you up."

"No, no. You can't ask the host of a party to drive you around town. It's pathetic."

She laughed it off. "Nonsense. We've always thought very highly of you. We didn't see you at the wedding either."

"Ah, well..."

"But let me guess...you just flat-out refused to come to that one, didn't you?"

I chuckled to myself. "What would make you think that?"

"Oh, just a hunch," she smiled and nodded. "A lot of single young men failed to make the wedding. But you know how that goes."

"Just out curiosity, Vicki, when did Sarah meet her husband?"

"About...eight months ago."

"So just a couple of months after the graduation ceremony. Right. So...probably not a great window of opportunity there."

She caught sight of my quick-but-sad half smile and sent me a reassuring glance. "I know how you felt about her, Henry," she said cautiously.

"Oh...well...I guess it's not much of a secret. Did she ever know?"

"Well...she may have known, but I don't think she really 'knew'. I guess it's a teenage girl type of thing."

"Hmmm. So at least I don't have to worry about the whole, 'Did she ever love me sort of thing?'"

Vicki stared at me in seriousness. "Henry, she never even knew you. She knew you played with cards. We knew about your magic act. Of course, I remembered you from years and years ago, when your mother used to babysit Sarah."

"Ah, right, I forgot all about that."

"You march to the beat of a different drum, Henry. It may take a while for you to meet someone really special. But don't give up. I used to think there was no one for me...but then I met Bill." She smiled joyously. "And I became a believer."

"There's a rumor going around that I am an intellectual. Maybe that's why I have trouble relating to girls my own age."

"Well there's that, and the cloak you wear...and all the dark arts?"

"Ah, true," I nodded in begrudging acceptance.

"We used to know a man like that. He was very intellectual, very smart. And yet a bit shy."

"Oh. And what's his story?"

"Well...he really didn't have any friends. And eventually he died. Lonely and alone."

"Ah," I said in confusion, but still nodding at whatever her point was.

"Yeah," she said sweetly. "You remind me a lot of him."

"Great!"

We laughed before saying goodbye and parting ways. At the time, I considered it serendipity. But as the weeks passed and nothing more became of Sarah, Vicki, or my two-bit magic show, I reevaluated the incident and now consider it a case of cruel irony. What better way to taunt the dead-inside apprentice than to wave Sarah's calm and understanding mother in my face—the wonderful and caring mother-in-law I could have had!

Alas, all bad memories, just like the good ones, eventually fade away into simple words. Sure, I was angry for at least another five years after the ironic happening. Sarah got married, had children, while I remained single, dabbling into mind spells and hypnosis, trying to make sense of the world and my strange powers one day at a time. Your perspective at twenty-seven has a way of changing a bit from when one is a teenager. A fellow's mind opens up and accepts new possibilities that a teenager cannot fathom in all of his idealism.

When I was very young, everything seemed to be about me. But now in my prime, I can see more of the world.

The next time I ran into Vicki Collins, years removed from the last encounter, the conversation went very differently.

"Hello, Henry," Vicki exclaimed as she hugged me. We were attending a cookout get-together for mutual friends. Vicki looked surprisingly good for all that had happened to her. Now in her 40s and wearing eyeglasses—but still with the same youthful face and tender smile I remembered—she looked much less mousy and more confident, slightly more sophisticated. Her clothes were also of exquisite quality, wearing a floral white dress in lightweight silk with a floral border of satin. Her bodice was draped for an elegant wrap around look and a knot at the waist.

Indeed, she was sophisticated. She had come into some money after Bill died in a work-related injury. Still, her well-preserved smile was a bit more affected than I recall. She had a widower's grief and perhaps even a twinge of resentment buried in the lines of her face.

"Wow, you look different," I said politely, noticing the slight personality change...though several years, a lost husband and grandchildren does tend to cause change.

"Yeah, that's what everyone tells me."

"How's Sarah?"

"She's good. She's chasing after the kids making sure they stay out of trouble."

"Ah...wow, I mean, you've changed a lot," I said again, apparently not over-thinking my gut reactions.

"Hahah...I guess I have. So are you still practicing magic?"

"Occasionally. I guess I've moved on from the kiddie stuff though."

"Oh really?"

"I'm going after more archaic knowledge. Spells, visions, hallucinations, whatever you call it," I said with a tightened smile and a giggle.

"Well, I was always very impressed with your talent."

"Thanks."

"I see you've ditched the cloak and are going more mainstream now," she said sardonically, noticing my suit pants and buttoned gray shirt.

"Well, nothing to prove anymore, I suppose."

I couldn't help but look despondent, thinking about Vicki's loss, and the strange set of circumstances that begat our friendship. "So do you still believe, Vicki?" I asked forwardly.

She hesitated a moment, thinking back to our discussion years ago, and then she answered proudly. "Yes, I do. I do, Henry."

We hugged each other goodbye and I retreated to a restroom.

I still couldn't shake Vicki from my mind. A woman who was kind enough to be there for me in my hour of need, and yet a woman I was fully incapable of helping in return. If I only I could do something for her, bring Bill back from the dead, cast a spell of good fortune, give her healing powers from within.

I decided that Vicki Collins, my friend, was deserving of a good spell. But rather than predict her good fortune or smite her enemies, I figured that she deserved to feel the same maddening love she believed in to the very end. Let nothing cloud your idealism, Vicki, or so I thought, as I cast a love spell upon her in secret.

I chanted in Aramaic while holding an image of her tender smile fresh in my mind. Then I proceeded to cast the love spell upon the lonely widower. "Love the way you deserve to love. Let not the cruel world pass you by. Refuse to be lonely. Fall in love truly, purely, eternally, just the way you imagined it would be. I command you to fall in love with the next man you meet. Let him keep you warm at night."

I waved my hand adding a special stipulation just for my dear, sweet Vicki. "And make sure that no one ever dares to break Vicki's tender heart. Whomever lands eyes on her first, will never leave her...will never resist her...will make passionate love to her all day and night. He will be transformed into her love slave and will taste honey whenever he kisses her lips."

I quickly left the house after casting my spell, anxious to escape the scene of the crime, but still somewhat curious as to whom Vicki would end up with; perhaps Leonard, the nice single gentleman and our mutual friend? Whoever the poor chap is, I thought, he is sitting prey just waiting to be snatched up.

The night was young so I decided to go pay my mother a visit. As I turned the corner of the street and parked, I noticed someone emerging from the porch. I turned the car off and exited, looking up to see who could possibly be meeting mom in the PM hours.

Imagine my shock when I saw Vicki Collins coming down the porch steps and looking at me in confusion—her pupils dilating and her voice taking on a strange, almost inebriated tone. "Hennnry..."

She stared at me for a long moment, as if second-guessing her instincts.

"Wh-What are you doing here?" I said, a sinking feeling coming over me, as I realized I was quite possibly the very next man she met after the spell was cast.

"I came to see your mom. I had something to give you."

She stared into my eyes again. Oh shit, I thought to myself. The spell was definitely working. In all the years we had known each other, she never once stared at me that way...not for that long, or without flinching.

"Oh Henry..." she giggled, suddenly acting flighty, and with a bit of a frog in her throat.

"Oh Vicki..." I said nervously, hoping maybe, just maybe, she saw someone before leaving the party.

She laughed again, this time a sexy, throaty, and breathless laugh. "Has anyone ever told you that you look a little like David Copperfield?" she asked, peering into my eyes and holding her hands on her hips.

"Who?"

"He's a musician!" she protested. "Don't make me feel old, Henry!"

"You're not old," I laughed respectfully. "You're still very pretty."

That was the wrong thing to say. She stared at me longingly after that remark, with a look that screamed "love me" and "I want to jump your bones" at the same time.

Suddenly, I felt a shift in the air, or maybe a slight alternation in color. I started to become very, very aware of

Vicki's breasts, which she held out firmly for me to see, tucked away behind that inviting white bodice. The temperature became hotter and a restless feeling came over me, traveling from my toe-curling feet all the way to my radiant hands.

I smelled the distinctive scent of Vicki's wetness, and as I did, I instantly felt my cock growing hard. I looked over at Vicki's quizzical face and felt the swelling intensify—so hard that it hurt. The spell was overpowering me and all I could think about was having sex with her, for hours, for days and nights. This virtual Viagra spell I cast was much too intense...so intense in fact that I couldn't even hide my huge erection from her. It was pushing through and out of my pants, dangling in front of her, and doing a little dance.

She looked down at my excitement and then back to my face, coyly smiling at me. "Henry...I don't want to be alone tonight."

"Vicki..." I said hesitantly, trying to fight the spell and my own raging prick, "I don't think we should do this."

The moment I said that, my cock head began swelling again, unnaturally hard, as if sucked through a pump.

She reached over and kissed me tenderly on the cheek and then moved over slightly to my mouth. Sure enough, her mouth scent tasted just like honey. Her weathered but still beautiful face was a huge turn-on, especially her glazed eyes, which despite all the witchcraft, still remained exceptionally kind.

"Vicki..." I sighed, losing control of my own senses and feeling the restless spell coming over me full force. "I need to make love to you... Right now, or as soon as possible."

She listened and felt the same passion, licking her lips for me, desiring to feel another kiss. "Let's go," she whispered. Probably a good idea since I was right outside my mom's house.

I left my car there and rode with Vicki, who was speeding like a demon on the ride back into town. The car ride home was intense to say the least. Her feminine scent was all over the car, and she was getting wetter by the minute. And all the while I was talking like a madman.

"Oh hurry...hurry...god, I want to make love to you. I want to make love to you...I need to feel it...I need to feel you...oh god Vicki...I want to make love to you!"

My cock was so hard for Vicki I was rambling on feverishly, speaking on pure emotion, high on love.

She turned and looked at me, that vicious look that says, "I'm going to let you stick it anywhere," and volunteered a great idea.

"I want you to come home with me. No one is there. Sarah and the kids are out of town."

"Yes! Yes! Yes oh god yes!" I said, just a tad enthusiastic.

She invited me inside and didn't say much after a very brief house tour. Neither of us knew what we were feeling or doing. All we knew is that the emotion, the lust, the love, and the adrenaline in our bodies was hitting a peak.

We French-kissed at the front door for a few moments, but it was hardly enough. My body needed to make love to her, and in her mind, she was already seeing stars, convinced that I was her one true love.

I knew the sex was going to be intense, but Vicki—my dear sweet friend Vicki— just about gave me a heart attack. From the moment she opened her dress to me, showing me her white bra and cute little breasts that were still very supple, I had to gasp for breath.

I put my face in her glorious bosom and found my way to ecstasy. She pulled down her bra cup showing me her erect nipple.

"Oh Henry..." she cooed as I sucked it oh so tenderly. I caught her making the face. The "tender", no teeth, eye-grinning smile that Sarah always used to have.

As if reading my sick mind, Vicki conjures up a wicked idea.

"Follow me. I want to show you Sarah's old room", she said with a head tilt.

I followed her one full room over to

Sarah's old bedroom. The bed and the wallpaper were practically untouched since Sarah's graduation and still looked like a high school student's room.

She lay on Sarah's pink and violet bed, spreading her legs for me and lifting the skirt to show me her pure white undies. She left her bra on for me with the exposed nipple showing, and so slowly, so torturously, unbuckled my pants.

I slid off my boxers and pulled out my hard, veiny penis—a sight for sore eyes indeed, as sex-deprived Vicki enjoyed fondling it with her hands, admiring its shape and contours.

I gently pulled her underwear down and looked longingly at Vicki's hairy mound, hiding one wet and wild chamber below.

"Oh Henry...put it in...put it in," she cried nervously, desperately and with teeth-clinching excitement.

"Oh Vicki...let me make love to you ... Ooohhh Vicki!" I shuddered in heat, as I felt her moist opening welcome in my aching cock.

"Oh! It feels so good..." she squealed, feeling every last inch of it plunge deeper inside.

I plucked away at her intimate, delicate parts, and my cock wouldn't stop swelling, no matter how much wetness she drenched me in. I felt a great feeling of peace come over me as I realized I was deep inside Vicki Collins' vagina. It was the closure I always wanted.

"Ohhh!" she screamed in zest. "Don't stop! Keep going. Just like that! Like that—!" she said with a voice crack and a whimper.

"Vicki...I just want to say..." I almost apologized to her, even in the midst of all that thrusting. I should have apologized for the reckless spell I enchanted. Or that I was going along with it, unable to resist my own shameful desires. But all I could really think to say at the moment was...

"You're so wet!"

"Mmm-hmm!"

And sure enough, my cock was soaked in Vicki's feminine juices. I avoided looking at her tender little face and instead glanced down to see the destruction—her petite little cave being pummeled by a ruthless red cock. I'm really glad she enjoyed the rough entry because I don't think I could have possibly stopped myself.

"Oh my god! Don't stop Henry! Keep going! Faster! Ooooohh!"

She never swore, just like the good mother she always was, but was oh so nurturing.

"Look at it...look at it..."

She knew how much her beautiful, naked body turned me on. As sweet, sweet torture she made watch as my wet cock disappeared inside of her, and then came back out, brushing against her wet bush. I saw it all. I saw and felt every last inch of her sex.

"Ohh Henry!" she groaned. "I'm close...cum with me."

"Where do you want it?"

"On my tummy," she said so innocently, so adorable.

I intensified my thrusts just enough so that I could finish right along with her.

"Oh Henry!" she screamed hard, grabbing my stomach and whatever other skin she could clutch.

"I-I can't hold it...!" I screamed.

I whipped it out and held it above her stomach. Just in time. I ejaculated all over Vicki's tummy and down to her pubes and thighs.

Oh Vicki. This wasn't what I had in mind for today. Shooting a load all over your crush's mother is not really good therapy. It's wrong. It's an accidental relationship all the way.

And yet, as much as I wanted to run away and explain my transgression in a tell-all letter...I was surprised by the peaceable and warm-hearted feelings I still had for Vicki. I still wanted to make gentle love to her...for hours...for days...for the rest of my life. Maybe it was the spell. Maybe I just like older women. Or maybe it's just revenge against Sarah.

Whatever it is...My magic practicing days are over.

8 MY AFFAIR WITH AN AMERICAN ECCENTRIC

My name is Alena. I am from the Czech Republic. One year ago, I came to live in America. My departure from my home country was to take place under strict orders of confidentiality. It is also the first thing everyone here wants to know about me. The second thing they want to know is if my hair color is naturally black.

I have always dreamed of coming to visit America and experiencing its culture and excess. The fast food, the theme parks, the landmarks, and the wide diversity of people. However, due to financial trouble, all I have been able to see so far has been local attractions—like bakeries, art festivals, and musical acts. I am not one to complain, however.

I do find art inspiring and music very refreshing to the soul. The artists in America remind me very much of my contemporaries in Prague. They are uninhibited and speak with their soul. Above all, they dream. I never thought much about American dreaming. I thought to live in such a country would be a dream come true.

But the Americans dream with intensity. They dream so hard and desire so much.

Now that I am here, on permanent stay, I begin to miss the little things of my home—most of all, the puppets and marionettes, which have an antiquated charm all of their own. Yet, I do not see anything quite like them here. Everything here is big and of great technology. The charms are missing.

I was put up in a small apartment and was told to find a job as a cashier at the local Doll Mart, who hires everyone, first come, first serve. Grasping the dollar money system was easy, but making small talk with the American public proved to be difficult.

"I detect an accent. Where are you from?"

"Czech Republic."

"Oh! That must have been fun, huh?"

I smiled in respect.

"I don't know much about that side of the globe. I imagine you have had a very difficult life. Lots of fighting. The Troubles. The IRA. Tragic."

I looked at him in confusion.

"You know what Tolstoy said about war. 'War—Oh mercy, mercy me, oh things ain't what they used to be.'"

I did not recall Tolstoy ever writing that before, but the American eccentric assured me of such.

"Can you read English?"

"Yes."

"Just wondering."

"Of course, I read English. If I did not, how could I work here and handle this money?"

"Dollars and coins are not literature," he said pedantically.

I nicknamed the peculiar man the Eccentric because he dressed like an American tourist even though he was in his own country. He wore very colorful clothing, like a peacock. His hair was long and curly, a bit mad, and of a thick brown color. He was older than I, a man in his mid-thirties, and with a larger frame but a body of imperfection. I was merely a girl of nineteen docile years. Whenever he spoke, I listened, even though I soon discovered his wisdom to be questionable.

"Hello again."

Him again. I nodded in politeness but

was quickly going tired of his visits.

"Did you know that Tolstoy liked pizza?"

"What?"

"It was his favorite American food."

I smirked back at him. "Now I know you are joking."

"Why are you such an ardent follower of Tolstoy?"

"Tolstoy was a brilliant man. What do you know of great literature?"

"What do you know?" he asked arrogantly. "Are you still going to school?"

"I am saving enough money so that I can go to school," I said to him firmly.

"And take what?"

"Creative writing."

"Ah, so you're a student. It's no wonder you admire Tolstoy. He was a great student himself."

I felt angry at him, but decided not to provoke him further.

As much as I wanted to ignore him and pack his disgusting groceries and shoo him away, I felt compelled to ask him more.

"And are you a writer? Is this why you develop this attitude?"

"I am a writer. But I believe in true visionaries. Like Jack Kerouac and Hunter S. Thompson."

"All writers have much to share."

"Not as much as you think."

I grimaced at him as I sacked a bag of

tampons and some chips and soda pop. "Have a nice day," I growled.

"Is that your natural hair color?"

I stared at him for a moment before going on to the next customer.

The next time I saw the Eccentric, he brought along with him another woman, presumably his spouse or girlfriend. I thought it would be likely that he would be quieter and more respectful, but I presumed wrong.

"Another author I admire is Allen Ginsberg. Ever read anything by him?"

"No, I have not," I said as I bagged the groceries. I caught his girlfriend looking at me, trying to figure out what our dynamic was. Perhaps thinking I was the "other woman"?

However, his wife was friendly and did attempt to speak to me kindly.

"Hey, you got new glasses, didn't you?" he said nicely, noticing my new frames.

"Yes, I did." I posed for him and his girlfriend, tilting my head and smiling.

"Beautiful!" he said, startling both his significant other and me. I retreated back into silence and sacked their groceries quickly.

The next time I saw him, his girlfriend was not present, but he was wearing a black beret, which I found to be rather suited to him.

"Hi there."

"Hello," I said shyly. "Nice hat," I said, making small talk and admiring his profile, a fitting portrait of the American artist.

"It's to remind the world I am an artist."

"Are you?" I said with a smile.

"I am. And all art is created in the admiration of beauty. I am inspired by only the most beautiful women. And you, my friend, inspire me."

I giggled but folded my arms. "You are saying I am beautiful?"

"I have said it and I will say it again."

"Well, thank you," I said with a tired laugh.

"But who am I? You probably get hit on all the time. Especially with that luminous, flowing hair and those adorable frames."

"Sometimes I do."

"If you want to learn how to be a writer, I can help you. Come with me later this week. We'll go out for coffee."

I raised my brow as I sacked his TV dinners. "You are inviting me out with you? Don't you have a girlfriend?"

"I do. But I don't know if she's ready to have coffee with you yet."

I laughed in his face. "Well, I do not think she would be inclined to meet me."

"She already met you."

He stared at me, startling me with his lustful eyes. I had never seen them before and they were frightening in their hunger.

"I cannot do that," I said softly to appease him.

"Why? Every day, men ask you out and speak of your beauty. You turn them all down because they can't do anything for you. They don't know where you come from. But I know you. And I know what you are looking for?"

"Oh? What am I looking for?"

He paused as he paid his bill with a credit card.

"You need a teacher. You need an education in literature and in creative thinking."

"I am not going anywhere with you if you have a girlfriend," I said in spite.

"What if my girlfriend was with me? Would you come then?"

"I...I don't know." I handed him his receipt. His time with me was finished.

"Thank you, my beauty from the Czech Republic."

I snapped back at his smug little face. "That is another quibble. Why do you say you love me if you do not even know my name?"

"I didn't say I love you. You won't even let me get to know you. And hey, you never asked my name either."

I ignored him but accepted what he said. His continued presence was making me more uncomfortable and yet more curious.

He came the next week, right on schedule, this time with his cute girlfriend accompanying him. This time his words were few and his voice was clipped in tone. But his eyes were on me for the entire transaction. He was speaking to me in silence, wanting me to consider his proposal.

At one point his girlfriend walked away to find another item. He made sure she was out of hearing distance and spoke to me frankly.

"I dreamed of you last night."

I rolled my eyes and remained silent.

"But dreams are nothing but shameful. They are subconscious thoughts, of no great consequence. No matter what Freud believed. Dreams don't mean shit."

I tilted my head in confusion. I was not sure what he wanted from me...although I did catch him ogling at my breasts and my backside as he was leaving.

On the next few times I saw him, I was not working the register. I was merely standing in the aisles or stocking items. But I always saw him out of the corner of my eyes, still watching me, still admiring my beauty, and still dreaming of what he desired.

I couldn't help but look back at him, just to see what his eyes were saying. His knowledge and his passion affected me. I found myself thinking about him, even hours after I saw him leave the store.

The next time he spoke to me, he was alone and seemed despondent in tone.

"Is everything all right?" I had to ask the Eccentric, usually a very animated man, who was suddenly quiet.

"Well...my girlfriend left me."

"What?" I asked in surprise.

"I don't know where she went. I don't know what I did wrong."

He seemed genuinely heartbroken, a new side of him I had never seen.

"I am sorry to hear that." I looked at him in compassion, even as he avoided my eyes. His confidence was shot. He was humbled.

"I am off work in about twenty minutes. Would you like to go somewhere?"

"I would," he said with a frown.

In less than two hours, we were back in my apartment and he was clutching my cheeks and kissing my chest upon my bed. A voice in my head said we were moving too fast, but the drinks from the bar and my seventeen months of loneliness argued with the thought.

I took off my work jacket and he began unbuttoning my shirt, yearning to uncover the treasures underneath.

"Oh Alena, you're so beautiful," he exclaimed as he saw my red brassiere. He moved so fast and yet he made all the right moves, caressing my face with his hands, entering his mouth with his fingers. He pulled my top down so he could find the nipple and suck it—not too hard but not too soft. He took possession of my body and I enjoyed his power.

I intentionally kept the lights dim so that his features were obscured. I wanted to know what it was like to make love to a stranger. He had not told me his name up to this point, only asking mine, but touched my body intimately as if he knew me.

I allowed him to undress me, one strip of clothing at a time. He didn't get a perfect view of me because of the dim lights, but I let him feel my nakedness with his mouth, his lips, and his wandering hands. He was a very patient lover, which was a surprise to me given his impatience in other matters.

When I was naked, he turned me on my belly and kissed my backside. He demanded that I call it "my ass" since this was a turn-on to him. I loved the feeling of his lips caressing my entire body, from my hips to my cheeks and up to my back. When he began kissing the back of my neck, my loins became warm for him and my heart raced.

I sighed softly as he began exploring my womanhood with his hands. He caressed my wet lips with his fingers and kissed my pleasure button softly. He licked it as lovingly as one did with ice cream and enjoyed whispering my name as I moaned in indulgence.

He stopped and sat up for a moment, coming closer to my face. "Do you trust me, Alena?"

"No," I said giggling.

"Trust me...."

He put two fingers deep inside of me and reached up. Then he began thrusting his fingers violently inside and outside of my muff. I instantly tensed up, feeling deep inner bliss and beautiful wet release.

"Aggh!" I screamed out much to my embarrassment. The intensity was climbing and I began to feel frantic.

"It's okay," he assured me, keeping up the fast pace.

"It's too much.... I can't...."

"Just let it happen.... Don't fight it...."

"Oohhhh!" I howled out as I rudely squirted fluid all over my lover's hands.

I gasped for breath, my heart still pounding from a frightening climax.

"I have never felt that before!"

"You live and you learn."

"I am sorry. That has never happened. Would you like to wash your hands?"

"No. I would not. I want your scent all over me. Your beautiful scent, Alena."

He reached over and kissed me on the neck.

"Why won't you tell me your name?" I asked in frustration.

"Because you don't care what my name is, do you?"

I said nothing. I did want to know him...but I was afraid at the intensity of what might be discovered.

I squinted my eyes in annoyance. There the Eccentric was back at checkout, once again accompanied by his girlfriend.

"How have you been?" he said with a devilish smile. His oblivious girlfriend helped him to stack groceries. I imagined that she did not suspect anything, as my cold demeanor towards him was nothing new or conspicuous.

"Oh, how much was this by the way?"

He boldly handed me a note in front of his girlfriend.

I WANT TO TASTE YOU.

I ripped the note up and threw it in the trash.

"Five ninety-nine," I said, staring daggers at him.

I gave him his receipt and took my break, not saying another word.

I went to the bathroom lounge and waited by the door, thinking about how easily I was deceived. I felt burdened, as if something was wrong.

But before I could enter the women's restroom, he appeared, grabbing me by the back and taking me into the men's restroom by force.

"You bastard! What are you doing?"

"I said I want to taste you."

"Get out of here! You are a liar."

"Slap me. It'll make you feel better."

I did slap him and I slapped him hard across the face. As soon as I did, I started to feel echoes of my past pleasure and a delightful swelling in my loins.

I reached out and kissed him with venom, and he responded by chomping on my tongue and putting his hands down my pants.

"What are you doing, you idiot?"

"You want to come again. I know you do."

"Wait! We cannot do this here...."

He took me my force and moved me into a bathroom stall, locking the door behind us. He took my pants off quickly and ripped the undergarments from my body in contempt. He sat me down on the toilet but took my legs into the air over his shoulders. This time the lovemaking was different. The lights were bright and everything was in full detail. When he unzipped, I saw every inch of his penis as it penetrated my sacred place. We both saw the act. I heard every last gasp clearly and witnessed his every shake and contraction until the very end when he climaxed inside of me.

"Oh, Alena!" he screamed, as he exploded into my inner regions. I watched it happen and watched as his firm member lost its power and shape, releasing it all into me.

I desired him so much I was powerless to resist. I didn't yet know his name. And that aroused me to the point of madness.

He pulled it out of me and stuffed it away, leaving behind my exposed nakedness and his warm seed inside of me.

"Where are you going?"

"My girlfriend is waiting in the car," he said flippantly.

"Bastard!"

He spared me a dramatic encounter by fleeing the bathroom before I could even sit up to scream at him.

"I'm sorry," he expressed, waving his hands and exaggerating his emotions.

The next time he saw me, he pleaded for forgiveness. He showed up and tried to communicate with me beyond my cold and locked façade. I stuffed his items into a single bag, not giving him the privilege of eye contact.

"It was my own mistake. I got greedy," I said to the air.

"No. It was mine. Like Lord Byron and Ernest Hemmingway, I am a man of sin. I see beauty and I must have it...experience it. Sometimes I get too carried away."

"It was my own fault for getting involved with a man who would not even tell me his own name."

"You didn't want to know."

"I did. As soon as I agreed to go with you, I wanted to know you. But now I know too much."

"What? You think you 'know' me just from what happened?"

"I know the type of man you are. And I cannot respect you."

"You don't know me that well, Alena. Did you know that I confessed everything that happened to my ex-girlfriend the same night? I promise you this. You will not see her around anymore. I was selfish, yes. But I took responsibility for what I did."

I shrugged off his defense.

"Besides," he said, turning his head and keeping his eyes locked on mine, "who are you to judge me? You didn't want a serious relationship either. You wanted it to be anonymous. No names. No strings or obligations. You wanted to learn."

He was correct in his analysis and he deserved my full-eyed attention. "Yes. I did learn. You were a good teacher."

"What would it take for you to give me another chance? To take you to my ex and show you that we are completely finished?"

What would it take to earn my trust? I, a girl from Prague who has no history, no real home, and no hope of ever going back? I do not know what this man or any man could do to earn my trust.

"What is your name, my eccentric American friend?"

"Cody...er, Codelaine."

I nodded and smiled. "It sounds like the name of a fictional character."

I handed him the receipt and looked into his eyes, still associating his face with my orgasm and remembering how his every knowing touch felt against my sensitive skin.

The truth is that I was not angry at him. I was not angry at myself. I was guilty of my own form of dishonesty—by using his cheating as an excuse to break away our engagement. It is possible that I knew all along he had a girlfriend and that he was manipulating his way into my bedroom.

But I desired it. He provided me with the learning experience I needed, and now I look bravely into a new world, without boundaries or limitations; with this, I have gained much more experience as to why people behave the way they do and why they dream so hard. I am young and in a free country. Nobody knows why I am here or if black is my natural hair color. But these are the mysteries that make creative lives interesting.

9 MEET AND DITCH

If I were to describe myself, I would call myself Debbie the Great. I would also call myself a "gorgeous" thirty-two-year-old woman, but gorgeous in an unconventional way. I have blonde hair and big natural boobs. But then again, I only believe in putting on makeup if we're going out. When I do wear makeup I paint my eyes dark, like zombie dark (I don't know why) and I curl my hair shamelessly.

I like the au natural look, and yes, I even wander the house naked most of the time. Sometimes I put on clothes. Say, if we're having over a very important guest over. Of course, if it's a guest we really like then maybe I would just be naked anyway. A house tour is so much better when the hostess is naked.

I'm kidding, of course. I am happily married to a wonderful guy named James, who is one of those guys boldly pushing ahead his midlife crisis by working out, hosting an Internet radio show, and driving around in his big-dicked sports cars. James has a nice clean face, short hair, and a tattoo on his bicep. The tattoo is of a bumblebee. Why? Because when he first met me, he tried to tell me that my name in Hebrew means "bee." I don't know if he was full of it or not, but we loved the running joke so much that he got a tattoo of a bee the weekend before our Vegas wedding.

And while I would never think about cheating on James, I have to admit our sex life has been in a rut lately. I don't know why. I guess after so many years of the old in and out, and seeing each other at our worst, we just lost the fire somewhere. How I do remember the first time we made love. Vividly! We were so hot and horny for each other we had sex in the backseat of his old Camaro.

So what happened? I'm not blaming our baby. Yes, I have had a child. No, I am not disclosing his age, name, or importance in this matter. Yes, I have stretch marks. Yes, I still look damned good for all I've been through.

So anyway, James and I had the big talk a few weeks ago. It really sucks because when you're being accused of being a sexual cold fish, it hurts so much, and yet it's real honest emotion coming from someone who loves you dearly.

"I don't know, I guess I'm just bored of the way we do it. We have no imagination anymore. It's just in and out. Like changing a diaper or doing dishes."

"Interesting to know how you feel about me sexually. Almost as exciting as changing a diaper or doing dishes. I feel smoking hot now!"

We sighed, stroked our heads, yanked our hair, and sat up-sat down repeatedly, going through the motions of the Big Relationship Problem.

"Don't put this whole thing on me. When is the last time you ever wanted sex? Usually it's me doing all the tapping and hinting around. Then you cave to the pressure, let me do you missionary, and then we fall asleep."

He had a good point. I don't know why or when exactly sex lost its allure. Maybe the kid ruined everything down there. Or maybe the two of us working a full-time job just takes its toll. Or, who knows, maybe the whole idea of marriage is a sham and we should be out having awesome sex with other people.

"Do you want to go out and have an affair?"

"I don't know," James said. "It seems a

lot more fun that it turns out to be."

"Well, how about this? Let's go out to a nightclub. Get dressed up nice. Put on your most charming attitude. And we can flirt with whomever we want."

"Hmm...and then what?"

"Then...I guess we have a decision to make."

James thought it over. The flirting with danger routine works every time. And by "works," of course, I mean it totally works by ruining good relationships, each and every time. Honestly now...who has ever benefited from flirting with other people? Maybe I just suggested the idea as a test to James, or even to myself, to see just how far we were capable of going outside our happy suburban marriage.

So we each got dolled up for Nightclub Nooky, our Friday night plan. I wore my sexy red party prom dress, complete with red band straps and ample cleavage. I curled my hair and wore my slutty eye makeup. Most of all though, I made sure I had the right look. The look that says "Hey, little boy...even if you could have me you wouldn't have a clue what to do to me."

James meanwhile went for the more

subtle approach—wearing a cotton suede blazer, jeans, and a cowboy hat. Sarcasm intended.

"You asshole, you don't even like cowboys!"

"True, but I've been perfecting my accent. 'Well, hey there little lady!' And besides, who cares what I think of cowboys. Women want to fuck cowboys."

I laughed his cowboy poetry off. "Well, good luck there, Buford Bud."

We arrived at the nightclub in the same car but the rule was already in place: once the car door slams, he doesn't know me and I don't know him. There is no secret word, no "saving each other" and no emergency time-outs. Whether I stripped in front of the entire bar, or James fucked another guy right in front of me, we agreed not to blow each other's cover.

The nightclub was intimidating at first, as the lights were pulsating and the dancing was aggressively rhythmic and provocative. I hadn't done a sexy dance in years...I honestly didn't know if I had it in me.

I don't think James was planning to cheat on me, nor I on him. I think our goal for the evening was to see who could score the most propositions in one night. Oh believe me, I was keeping count and I was going to win.

I sat down at the bar and turned on my

half smile—just eager enough but not quite begging for it. Within minutes, some elegantly dressed black man sat beside me and smiled.

"Good evening, beautiful."

"Hey there, bar patron."

"Actually, I prefer Jason."

"Jason? It sounds so conventional."

"I guess it is. Excuse me."

He dismissed himself and walked away. Damn. Proposition Number One blown. I wondered how James was doing.

James started getting chuckles as soon as he walked into the club, sporting that retarded cowboy hat of his. It wasn't technically fair...I'm sure I would have gotten more proposals had I worn a babushka hat and talked like "Natasha."

James played up the whole cowboy gimmick and pretended as if he was a big strong, oil-rich Texan straight off the dummy truck.

Within a few minutes of arriving, I saw him talking to two girls, probably just barely old enough to drink. They giggled as he did his cowboy material.

"Well, hey little lady," he said in his worst accent possible, "Maybe you should buy me a drink since you're feeling so generous!"

The girls giggled and poked him in the chest.

Damn. He was beating me. Time to get

serious and win this.

A younger guy, looked like surfer dude, decided to sit two spots down from me. Maybe he needed a buffer zone because he was definitely into me and started talking midway into a conversation. He was cute, if a little green, and had long blonde locks of hair, a small goatee growing and beady little eyes that were still very cute.

"So you know what I hate about surfing in a hurricane?"

"Um...what?"

"All those fucking lifeguards, dude. They suck balls. I say they should stop sending out warnings and give us freedom, man."

"Are you for real?"

"Shit, you want to see my board right now?"

"Your board?" I asked, raising my eyebrow suggestively.

I cracked up along with surfer dude.

"So what brings you here, pretty lady? You don't seem like the type that frequent this kind of dank very often."

"Oh just the same old story, I guess," I said, molesting my wine glass hoping he was paying attention. "Divorced. Feeling lonely. And trying to boost my confidence a little."

"You don't need any artificial boosts. Just look in the mirror and love yourself."

"I...have never loved myself while looking in the mirror."

We laughed again.

"No, seriously though. Self-worth comes from within, foxy lady. Age doesn't matter. You got a beautiful rack, smoking hair, and one sexy body."

"Wow! You're forward, you know that?" "My name's Manny, not forward. And that's how I live my life. I do surf through hurricanes. I live free and dangerously. When I'm not risking my life or doing something insane, I'm drinking hard and talking to drop-dead gorgeous women."

"Like me?"

"Well there ya go, you're already feeling more confident and full of yourself, aren't ya?"

James was making leeway across the room, every once in a while, turning my way and scouting out the windsurfer. I have to take James at his work on what happened next...I only know this conversation from what he told me. Honestly though, I can't imagine why he would hide something when his admitted conversation was as steamy as one could imagine.

Cowboy James talked to "Scarlet," a younger redhead with big eyes and even bigger titties. She was dressed like a total slut, packing heat in a shredded black dress with shredded arms, a scoop neckline, and a shredded cut-out front that practically shoved her naked tits into a man's face, except for the all-important nipples.

Scarlet was a maneater all right and seemed to sense James' money-like pheromones.

"So why are you really here? And why are you pretending to be a cowboy?"

"No good?" Jason asked, a tad disappointed.

"I admire your acting ability...but I just don't buy the accent."

"Oh phooey. And I thought I was going all Jon Voight with this getup."

"More like John Travolta."

"Is that bad?"

"A little bit. But I don't care. I find you interesting."

"Well...young lady, I find you interesting as well!"

She laughed, knowing full well James was staring at her boobs ripping through that shredded dress. "I'm sure you find me very interesting."

We talked to our respective temptations for almost an hour, learning about their life and admiring their spunky attitudes and gorgeous bodies. The more we talked to these sweethearts and carefully kept secrets about our real home life, the more we started to realize that cheating just wasn't very practical. We're all talk. We're chicken shit. We're old and married. Sad but true.

Of course, telling our two temptations—Surfer Dude and Slut Girl—that we weren't "serious" proved to be a little more troublesome than we thought.

James was led by Slutty Scarlet over to the private lounge, urging him that she had something important to say.

"I like you, James, because I can sense when guys are full of shit. And you're cocky. But you really have something going for you."

"You can sense that just from my face?"

"Are you really arguing me about this?"

"No, no. I accept the compliment."

"Actually, my theory on you is that you already have a wife. And you're coming here to be naughty."

"Huh..." James flinched.

"And I also think your wife is either a major prude or she has really small breasts. Because, dear sir, for the last thirty minutes you have been staring at my chest."

James nervously tilted his head and grabbed his cheek. "Umm...really? Did it seem that way?"

"Yeah. It did. So, Mister Rich and Successful Scoundrel...don't you want to know what they feel like?"

James swallowed nervously and took a few seconds too long to object.

She pulled the dress down by the shoulders and all the way down the neckline and to the chest, opening her huge honkers to him.

James was out like a light, stunned, and drooling, so he was pretty much helpless to stop her next move. She grabbed his hands and put them right on her bare tits, making sure his fingerprints touched her big, pouty nipples.

"Oh sweet Mother Mary..." he said.

"What do you think, Mister James?"

"Oh my god...they're not real...but who cares?"

"You want to get out of here?" she asked with a giggle and a hair toss.

"I...I...can't, Scarlet. The truth is, yeah, I got a lot of money and I still drive a Camaro. But I am still in love with my wife. She's here. We're just playing around."

"Oh I see," she said with a chin raise, but still not breaking her strong, stubborn eye contact. "Do you and your wife like company?"

"Oh Jesus," he said, looking over her big tits and pondering the possibilities. "I really hope so."

Meanwhile, I had gone outside to the parking lot, following Manny all the way to his creepy little white van.

"Is this the part where I get kidnapped?"

He scoffed. "Don't flatter yourself. You're the cougar. I should be afraid of you, hot mama."

We giggled a bit and then he dropped a bombshell. He opened his old Ford Ram sliding door, showing me all of his layers and layers of windsurfing equipment.

"Wow. This is really cool!" I said, not really understanding what I was looking at, but definitely in awe of his obsessive hobby.

"Yeah. Kind of leaves you speechless, huh?"

"Umm...yeah!"

"Yeah heheheheh," he tittered. "I'm just fucking with you. I only wanted to offer you a blunt."

"...You are fucking awesome, Manny!"

"I know, right?"

After smoking a doobie and sitting in Manny's passenger seat, I started to feel really good about myself, my age, the world, and even Manny's dumb stoner face. He started to look really, really cute and wild sex with a surfing hippie was not entirely out of the question. By our contract, I really had no obligation to remain faithful to James. My sleeping with another man would only bring the situation to a head—and we would have to make a "decision." Meaning I could probably do Manny, confess, cry about it, and get off scot-free.

Damn it, Manny (and his magic cigar) were making it so hard to leave and so hard to remember anything but my short-term memory.

"Say..." Manny asked innocently. "You want to kiss?"

"Why not?"

Manny leaned over to the passenger seat and kissed me on the lips. I was pleasantly surprised by his kissing ability—soft, but not afraid, strong, but mellow—and by the fact that he tasted like cherry vanilla vodka.

I broke the kiss after a long, steady moment. "Umm, Manny...the truth is I'm married."

"Yeah I kinda' figured."

"I'm happily married. We're just sort of playing around."

"That's cool. You soft swap?"

"No. No, we don't."

"Oh, bummer. So this is it?"

"Sorry..." I said, clenching my teeth, hoping he wouldn't flip out..

"Nah, it's okay, man. Tell you what though, if your hubby ever treats you bad, or like, dies or something, just give me a call, okay?"

Now that is a grand romantic gesture if I've ever heard one.

James and I finally broke away from our dates and met back in the red Camaro.

With my lips still tingling from Manny's smoky kiss, and James' hands still shaking from an anticipated (but rejected) idea of a threesome with big breasted Scarlet, we were so hot for each other!

As soon as we looked at each other, and well before the confessions came out, we tore into each other's faces like porn stars.

I kissed James hard, stuffing his mouth full of my tongue and crawling over to mount him like the little whore I felt like.

He went after my breasts like a horny teenager, pulling down my prom dress top and wiggling his lips all over my breasts and spicy red bra.

"Backseat, stranger?" he asked, hot and out of breath.

"No. Do me right here."

It was wild all right! He pulled my bra cups down, shoving my tits up and out into the open world. He attacked my nipples with his tongue, licking them hard and selfishly—just the way I like it in the backseat of a stud's car.

I straddled him, putting my knees down over his legs, and helped him whip that cock out like a good boy. He unzipped but I went digging for that big thing and stroked it up to proper size.

I lowered my pussy down on his manhood, enjoying his closing eyes, so relieved to feel my wetness.

"You didn't wear any underwear?" he

said as I bounced up and down, letting that hot rod penetrate me."

"Does that surprise you?" I looked into his eyes and French-kissed him. "Easy access. Anyone could have fucked me tonight. But I chose you."

"I'm glad it was me," he undulated, his voice cracking and his body shifting, moments away from the big one.

"Where do you want me...to come?" he asked, frantically resisting the splurge.

"Anywhere but inside me. Don't you dare...come inside me," I said firmly, looking down at his crying eyes while humping the fuck out of him.

"Oh! I'm coming!"

He shifted around violently, shaking the whole car, but his cock was all mine to torture. "Yeah! Give me that cum, baby! That's a bad motherfucker!"

He exhaled a huge pornographic scream as he shot his load deep into my pussy.

He gasped and recovered slowly. I stayed on top of him enjoying the sensation of his cock and balls shrinking down, and the wet, sloshy remnants inside of me.

"Oh my god, honey...we didn't even use any protection!"

"Oh Debbie...that's the kind of hard-core Camaro sex that makes accident babies totally worth it!"

So there you have it. That's how you

meet new people, ditch your dates and save a marriage. Maybe long-term monogamy is all about reckless love, never losing sight of your potential or opportunities. Or maybe it's about tolerance, as in tolerating our stupid cravings for bimbo attention.

Whatever the case...it really helps to have a Camaro.

10 THE LIFE MY MASTER ALLOWS ME

When you're a fulltime working mom, life is always so grand. I fulfill the housewife fantasy while I achieve the American dream. I work hard in the daytime. I pick up my son Dylan at daycare every weekday at 2 p.m. I go home, make dinner, and clean up just in time for my adoring husband to come home and kiss me goodnight. Oh yeah, and I shop till I drop on the weekends. No one ever told me Suburbia would be so much fun!

I look at myself in my rear view mirror driving the family SUV, which is a pretty shade of light blue, and full of predictables; baby clothes, work folders, old music CDs—for a CD player we don't have—and of course, plenty of hair curlers, combs, and scissors.

I admire the details of my reflection, the perfect image of the modern housewife, the pride, and joy of Louie, or "Pops" as we all call him. My blonde hair is immaculately styled and curled, made to perfection by my salon partner Wendy, who refuses to give her boss an employee discount. But like I always tell my customers, good hair is worth paying for.

"Hi honey," I reassure my hubby on the phone. "I'll be home in about an hour. I have to pick some things up at the store and then head over to work to lock up."

He reassures me so kindly. He is the near-perfect husband, punching a clock away from the house just long enough to make you miss him.

"I love you too." I think it's so funny that Dylan looks just like his dad. I can't help but smile at what a beautiful day it is and how great I feel...even as I pass up all these slow drivers and idiots who can't give me a simple turn signal. No, I'm not going to let them ruin my day. I am grinning ear to ear and I feel great. I look like a 30-year-old mom, but one that is thoroughly enjoying the day-by-day journey.

The phone rings. I know who it is. I try to ignore the aggressive little ringtone.

A chill comes over me, and I gulp down my thoughts of merriment. Maybe, if I just ignore it...it will go away.

It's becoming harder to keep a genuine smile. I can feel my face dissolving into shame, a forced smile, a polite smile, but mostly, a disquieted look of surrender. I look at my reflection in the SUV's vanity mirror. I wonder if it's enough.

My hair is perfectly styled, and my face is scrubbed to a perfect, porcelain-like glow. I am wearing a white floral dress with protruding white rose pedals, thin shoulder straps, and a black belt. The red jacket keeps me tucked away and warm from the breezy day.

But I don't know if it's enough.

I wasn't expecting to go anywhere but home today. The anxious, brutal feeling overwhelms me, and I feel my knee shaking, starting to hit the gas pedal. I better slow down and gather myself. I don't know if I can get out of this.

I shouldn't have worn this dress. The dress is nice, and it does make Louie happy, but it hides my DD cups too well. I'm not supposed to hide.

I hold my head in stress as the phone continues to ring.

I glance down at the caller ID text and my dread is confirmed. I'm having trouble breathing. I can't swallow away all the emotions. The expectations. The disappointment. The shame.

I sigh and hold my chest in comfort.

I am stuck in traffic so have no choice but to make the call, killing a few awkward, can't-concentrate-anyway moments.

He picks up and I shut my eyes.

"Hello?"

"It's Cassie." Nothing more needs to be said.

"Why didn't you pick up the second I called?"

"I'm sorry."

"You're sorry?"

"I was on the road..."

"That's no excuse, Cassie."

I remain quiet, as he thinks and ponders over my punishment. The ultimate sign of respect.

"I am walking Montgomery Street as we speak. I want you to come and pick me up.

"I can't do that."

"What?"

I'm not supposed to contradict him. I know. But I want to resist. "I can't, I'm not alone right now."

"Then leave whoever you're with behind."

He knows I'm bluffing. His strong voice echoes in my mind. His anger, his happiness, his joy and his disappointment, all equally fill me with the same internal aching.

"You know where I am, Cassie. Come and pick me up right now. I don't want to hear any discussion. Do you understand?"

"Yes..." I sigh in uncertainty. I can't be doing this right now. I'm so late. So unprepared. But I have no choice.

I coast through Montgomery Street taking my sweet time, hoping to postpone the inevitable. The butterflies are fluttering in my tummy, and my mouth is drying up from nervousness. Sometimes, I think I can't breathe properly unless he tells me how.

I see a handsome and familiar face from a distance. About my age, and with tall, dark features. He looks like he should be on the cover of a sexy men's magazine, all except for his eyes. They are unforgiving. Demanding. Insatiable. Destructive. They peer through my soul and make me shudder in retreat. Why does he have to look at me that way? Even from halfway across the block, I become too weak to stand and have to inhale through my nose to slow my breathing.

What does he want? He walks over, eyeing me the whole way and wearing a casual shirt with slacks. He is dressed for business. And his business, I fear, is me.

He enters the SUV and sits in the passenger's seat, glaring over at me at first, and then mellowing into an almost sickly calm.

"Did you think you could escape?" he asks, lowering his eyes in haughtiness.

"No."

"No, what?"

"No, master."

I blink my eyes and hide my face, already feeling the defeat. Once a master declares his slave, there is no going back. There is no resistance. All I can hope for now is that he is gentle...that he is kind...that he respects my boundaries.

"You've been avoiding me lately. What, is it your family? Your husband and child? Are those distractions getting in the way of your life here?"

"No, master." I can barely raise my face to him. "They are just distractions. I live the life that you allow me."

"Cassie..." he smiles. "The successful career woman. The working mom. The perfect 'housewife.'" He giggles quietly. "You really believe it, don't you? I think that's why you're avoiding my calls because you want to get away. You've deceived yourself into thinking you're a real person."

"But—"

"But you're not. You belong to me. Do

you hear me?"

"Yes."

"Yes, what?"

"Yes, master," I say, slightly strained, as the anxiety is traveling down my stomach and into my most intimate places.

"If they only knew what a whore you were."

"Yes," I sigh to him.

"If your husband only knew the truth."

"Yes..."

"Say it."

"No...please don't..."

"Say it! Cassie, are you a good little slave or a bad one? Do I have to report you to—"

"No! No!"

"Then say it. Tell me the truth your husband knows. And tell me how that makes you feel."

I hide my eyes in my hands, even as I try not to feel my heart pounding in my chest. I can't bear to look at my reflection as I say these things. But my master demands to hear it.

"My breasts..."

"No, your tits, Cassie. Say it."

"My tits...my tits belong to you."

"Why is that?"

"Because," I say, shivering with anticipation. "You bought them for me."

"That's right."

He lunges over and holds my face,

mangling my lips in his rugged hands. "And how does that make you feel?"

"Like a whore," I whimper.

"That's right. I bought those breast implants for my little titty whore. And now you think you're a mother?"

"No. I don't."

"Did I give you permission to start a family?"

"No, master."

"Pull into this parking lot here." My master points me to an empty parking lot right outside a tax building closed for the day.

"Why?"

"Don't ask why. Do it."

"But—"

"Cassie, you're not going to like what I do to you if you keep asking questions."

I stifle myself and await my master's orders.

He leers over at me and looks at my big DD titties. The ones he bought. Breasts only he has the right to admire.

"You have some nice tits, Cassie."

"Th—"

"Don't talk. Do as I say. I want you to take your jacket off."

"No...I-I can't. I can't do this here."

He sighs in disappointment and I hide my face in regret. "You still haven't learned anything. Have you? You've become self-important. You forgot where you came from. You forgot who you are."

I know that he's right. Maybe, I want to fantasize or imagine that I'm someone else. But everything my master says is true.

"Now take off your jacket. And let me see your blouse."

"Right here? Now? But there's still sunlight—"

"I'm not going to ask you again."

I shut my eyes in acceptance. I cannot question his will, even if it doesn't make sense to me. I avoid his eyes and look around outside, hoping no one is watching. I take off my red jacket, and notice my master ogling my tits, tucked away behind this blouse, no doubt piquing his curiosity.

"Please. Just let me go. Master."

"No, I don't think so. I might let you go. But first, you have to show me how sorry you are."

"No..."

"Right here, right in broad daylight...I want you to take off your blouse so I can see your bra."

I can't resist him. He knows this is too much. But I deserve it for abandoning him when he needed me. My breasts belong to him. My husband Louie doesn't know this dark secret. After I married Louie, my Master demanded that I get breast implants. Louie, the poor, naïve man, thought he was buying them for me. But I made sure to tell the doctor to wire the money from him, My Master, just before surgery, away from my husband. Never letting his sweet, dear soul know the horrible truth. That I'm a..."

"Whore. Yes, you're a good little whore housewife," Master whispered, watching me raise my blouse above my head. I strip down to my white lacey bra, jiggling my big tits, just the way he likes it.

"How does that make you feel?"

"Like a whore," I look into his eyes and find the strength to keep looking.

"Sitting there in a bra? Are you afraid of getting caught?"

"Yes."

He looks me over, wondering where my limits are. I am ashamed to say I have no limits with him. I feel the anxiety dissipating—only when he looks at my tits and thinks dirty thoughts. I am calmer, but warm and a bit flustered from his game.

"If I were to let you go right now...back to your 'family,'" he says with vicious sarcasm, "Where would you go?"

"I have to go shopping. At the mall."

"What for?"

"For clothing. For..."

"For who?"

"For my family."

"You really take your new life seriously,

don't you?" he asks with an evil cackle.

I can't have him disrupting my life. He is my Master, but it is permitted to live my life away from him, if approved by him. Maybe if I beg he will have mercy on me.

"Master...can I please go to the mall? Please? Your little whore is asking you."

He smiles...deceptively kind. He is going to let me go. But I shudder to think why he's letting me off the hook so easily...

It has been three hours since I dropped my Master off at his residence. I haven't gone home yet. I am much too agitated and confused. At what I am. At what my husband will think. At whether I am a whore pretending to be a housewife, or a housewife pretending to be a whore.

I try to distract myself by looking through clothing at a downstairs retail store. I am supposed to be shopping for newborn clothes, but maybe I should treat myself to a new dress or a housedress. Something comfortable that will help with the anxiety, the pounding, the expectation of what he's going to do to me.

And how much, to my shame, that I want it.

As I continue to look through the clothing, I feel an ominous presence come behind me. He sticks his hand up my dress and tugs at my underwear. I turn around—outraged as a mom—until I see Him there, standing, taunting, and waiting.

He's not done with me. He is going to make me suffer.

"What are you doing here?"

"Always with the attitude."

"I can't do anything here!" I exclaim in exasperation. I shouldn't be challenging my master, but I am torn between two worlds, and in between two stores that mirror my battle perfectly: the sexy lingerie store to my right and the baby clothes store right across from it.

"I think you can do whatever I set my mind to."

I look down in weakness and await his order, politely putting the dress back that I was sampling.

"I want you to follow me, Cassie."

"Why?"

"No words. Just follow me."

My suspiciously quiet and un-resentful master directs me outside the retail store, past the lingerie shop and right into the baby's clothes store. I can't imagine what he is thinking.

"Listen...what do you hear?"

I stand still and obey. I hear nothing at first, until I concentrate and hear that most alarming of noises. Another woman is in the store holding a baby. It is crying for milk. It's the worst possible thing that can happen to an innocent bystander mom.

I pause, remaining perfectly still, trying not to panic, and staring into his vengeful eyes.

"What's wrong?" he asks, leering at me in cruel pleasure.

"It's a strange side effect of pregnancy. My nipples leak when I hear a baby crying."

"I figured," he said, with a dire expression. "I want to see them. Your milky mommy tits. Show me. Right now."

"Right now? I can't!" I look around in desperation, looking for a place of retreat so I can indulge my Master's sick fantasy and spare my pride.

"Then you better find a private place. Fast."

I look around frantically, hoping to find a bathroom.

"Or I will tear your shirt off and expose your tits right here, in front of everybody."

"No..." I mewl, surveying the area.

I see something. I walk quickly over to the closest "private" area I could find, all the while ignoring my master's public spanking of my ass.

It's a photo booth, the mall's least private location, but the closest we were going to get to privacy given the circumstances.

My Master grabs my tits through my blouse and jacket and squeezes them merrily, hurrying my retreat. I feel a huge sense of excitement rush through my body, finally settling in my moist pussy. Some of it is adrenaline, some of it was the pain and the humiliation, and some of it is even the hatred the new me had for my old master. But he enjoys looking at my hateful expression. Every time I glower at him, it is enough to get him excited and violate my intimacy even more so.

He doesn't waste but three seconds after I usher him into the photo booth with me. He buries his hands inside my blouse, reaching under the bra just so he could grab my leaking nipples.

I sigh deeply, but back away. "Let me get undressed."

"Hurry up!" he yells, probably making the passersby outside a bit suspicious.

Even as I hurry to take pull off the sleeves of my jacket, my master still squeezes my breasts through my blouse, attacking my mommy parts as if they were something atrocious.

When I finally took off my jacket, he loses all patience. He grabs my white blouse and tore it right through the middle exposing my white bra and firm cleavage to him and anyone outside peeking in.

"Take it off! Take it off!" he rages, giving

a direct command to his slave.

I put my hands behind my back and unfastened the latch. He stands still, waiting for me to expose my tits to him. I pull it off and watch as my huge DD cups fall into perfect bouncy control. They are his to fondle. They are his to injure or destroy.

"These are some nice big mommy titties, Cassie."

"Yes."

"I'm jealous. Everybody but me is getting a taste of these."

"Do you want to taste them, master?"

He looks at me in disdain, never aroused by my dirty talk. He is only turned on by my silence. My grief.

"Play with your tits, Cassie."

"I don't know how..."

"Squeeze your nipples."

I shut my eyes in disgust. The slave in me is gushing with excitement, but the mother in me detests him. I have no choice for the moment, but to indulge my master and give him what he wants, that is, my obedience.

I squeeze my right nipple with my index finger and thumb, making it alert and hard for him. I do the same to the other one, letting him soak in my naked titties in all their used up and shriveled mommy glory.

He takes his time, reaching into to my

hot bosom and swallowing up the nipple.

I feel the heat of his mouth and moan in release. It feels so wrong, so dirty and cheap, but so wonderful. The nerves are calm; my mind is free and relaxed. My tits are right where they should be, in my master's mouth.

He sucks on them with disgrace, like an animal or a sex-starved maniac. He enjoys sucking them hard so he can taste my special mommy milk, lent to others but all for him.

As he licks up the emissions, I start to feel a pang of orgasm inside of me, in my inner parts, my breasts, my red face, and deep in my blood.

Only my master can ever make me come this way, and all without ever touching my lady parts. He only touches what he owns.

"Oh! Master..." I sigh loudly, against my own will, failing to keep our escapade quiet. "Suck my nipples..." I say as my voice cracks.

He starts to sigh, too, perhaps close to coming himself. To come in front of his slave would be a great dishonor. Not surprising to see him quickly exit the booth and make a break for it, probably holding down his rock hard cock from public view.

Now I remain in here, falling from near orgasm, my tits hanging out and milking and with only a jacket to cover them for the long ride home.

Why does my master do these awful things to me?

And why am I only happy when he's doing them?

It has been five days, and I still haven't heard anything from my master. I live in constant fear and pulsating anxiety in my head...always fearing that my master will surprise me when I least suspect it. That he will come and admit who he is and destroy my family.

Or my biggest fear of all...that he will never come back. That he will let me be a housewife and mother and no longer violate or humiliate me. If he offered today to leave me behind forever...and treat me like a respectable mother and career woman...I don't think I could let him go.

So which of us is really disturbed?

I look at myself in the bathroom mirror, wearing a sexy black dress and shawl that hardly covers up my master's bought and paid DD cups. I have to admit to myself, as I wipe away that maternal smile and embrace my whore lips, that sometimes, I dress for my master more so than Louie. Part of me hopes my master will come here, unexpectedly and punish me. With no boundaries or limits. No sense of decency.

The very thought of being dressed sexy for my Master, while being admired by Louie is sickening and is making my panties slightly wet.

"Are you okay, honey?"

"Yeah...just feeling restless, I guess."

I pace around the room, unable to just have a good time. My empire waist dress is romantic and yet spicy, with a sweetheart neckline and cap sleeves. I don't look like a mommy whore; I don't even feel like one. I feel like a sophisticated woman. I know who I am. I am invincible.

The doorbell rings and I instantly tense up, forgetting all my confidence in an instant.

"Who is it?"

Someone speaks outside. Louie has his hand on the door, no doubt ready to open it. I wish to myself that it's a neighbor, a friend, or even a policeman. Anything but...

"Rio's the name."

My master enters my house, making jolly small talk with my husband and taking in the scenery of my living room—a palace, a sanctuary he was never allowed to behold.

"Honey, this is Rio. I met him at work the other day," Louie says happily, not having the slightest cue his big titted wife is about to be punished and punished good. My pussy gets wet as I look into his mad and yet congenial eyes, playing his part perfectly. The throbbing sensation overtakes me. I know my master is going to give it to me and give it to me good—without restraint. I can only hope he's not going to blow my cover. He has the power and my life is his to create or destroy.

I listen in ecstatic agony, feeling the inevitability of my affair, but watching in horror as my master makes small talk with my husband and pretends to be genuinely interested in my career and my life as a mom.

"You're a great mom!" he says over drinks with Louie and I. "I'll bet you're very good at it," he says innocently, hiding missiles behind his dark eyes.

Every second my master isn't touching me or torturing me I grow all the more restless, wanting this build-up of tension to be released. I've never wanted anyone so badly. I'm afraid to say...if my master fucked me right here in front of my husband...I wouldn't object.

"Can I use your bathroom?" he asks innocuously.

"Yeah sure. Honey, show him where it is," Louie exclaims.

I squint my eyes in frustration. I was trying so hard to resist. To be a good wife to you, Louie. To be a good mother. Why did you make it so easy for me to fail?

No. I can't think like that. No one failed. I am simply giving to my master what he deserves. He doesn't ask much....

I follow him to the bathroom, and he can't help but turn to me and stare in sexy, mesmerizing menace.

"What are you going to do to me?" I ask in a mousey voice, just the way he likes it, as we stand outside the bathroom.

"You're a bad slave," he says, looking down at me in judgment. "If you were any good as a slave, I would have fucked you in secret." He looks around the hallway making sure his volume can't be heard. "But you haven't been obeying me. It's time to punish you."

"No...don't do this," I squeal silently, keeping my voice down from my clueless husband and sleeping son.

"Are you telling me what to do?"

"No...master...I'm not," I say as a cower away from his face.

"Get on your knees."

I listen and obey. He turns around to survey the area and then unzips his pants. I kneel on the floor, ready to give him anything he wants, and at whatever cost.

I watch in silence, shuddering, as he takes his hard cock out and shows it to me. Just as I lick my lips, my master corrects me.

"Stay still, you whore."

My master madly attacks my dress, pulling down the shoulders and wrenching it to my waist, my tits popping out for his amusement.

I look up at him in devotion, terror, and complicity.

"I didn't wear a bra today. I had a feeling you might come for these."

Without a word, he takes what is his with feverish delight. He grabs me by the shoulders and sticks his veiny, throbbing cock in between my tits.

I exhale, taking in his hard, stubborn, violent rage between my bosom, and dropping my mouth in passion.

But I have to keep quiet. My master crossed the line—he's titfucking me on the floor in our hallway, not even having the scruples to take me into the bathroom and do it in private.

All I can hear are our muted grunts and the sound of his cock sliding against my sweaty, moist tits.

We both look at each other as we notice my nipples are leaking again. He rubs his cock all over my nipples covering them in milky goo just so he can get a wetter tittyfuck. He continues clobbering my tits with that angry dagger, making them just as milky wet as my gushing pussy.

"Mmm..." I hear him starting to crack.

What an honor...my master is going to come on me. And in front of my family. "Ohh," he grunts, trying to keep it quiet but still making way too much noise for a quiet quickie.

He looks into my eyes and whispers. "Is this what you like, mommy? Being a slutty tit whore? You like getting those big milkers fucked?"

"Yes!" I say loudly, moments away from a nipple orgasm, totally careless as to who is listening outside.

I feel his imminence...his cumshot is going to be huge. His cock is already pumping and contracting, and his hairy balls are firming up, ready to unload. I don't even have to ask where he's going to cum. He wants to spread his seed all over my big mommy tits, defiling them for everyone else.

"Oh, shit!" he whispers in agony as he feels it building. "I'm going to cum on your tits, Cassie..."

I clench my teeth, already orgasming, and waiting to feel his glorious splatter.

"Cum on me, cum on me," I whisper in my best little puppy begging voice.

"Oh GOD!" I can't help myself...I let out one huge scream that I know my husband heard.

My master cums all over my big tits and makes me watch as every last big squirt and little droplet falls on my chest, creating an almost perfect W shape, as if to remind me I am a good little whore. Tainted, used, soiled, my dirty tits are now his property. Only to be used with my master's permission. He gets off of me, huffing and puffing from his own orgasm and staring me down. I watch his cock throbbing for a few moments, but eventually it loses its shape. He backs away from my kneeling position and puts his pecker away, zipping up smoothly.

But I remain frozen. He still hasn't told me what to do. I have cum all over my tits and am kneeling down with his cock scent still on me.

"You're a good slave, Cassie." He says, warming my heart.

"What now?"

"Get dressed. Go back to your husband and son. But don't shower. Wear my cum all over your tits for the rest of the night."

I know better than to resist his wishes. My mind objects and my moral mother compass finds it shocking. But my heart and my passions do not let me speak. Whatever my master commands, I do. This is the life he has allowed me, and I am grateful to him for sharing my body with the people that I love.

ABOUT THE AUTHOR

Readers: I want to expand a few of the stories to see where the characters can be explored further. If there are any of the stories that you would like to read more about again, I'd love to hear from you!

Visit my blog at www.breanakohr.com

Join my newsletter for free exclusive previews www.breanakohr.com/in

Follow me on Twitter at www.twitter.com/breanakohr

Like my page on Facebook at www.facebook.com/breanakohr

Discover my books at major ebook retailers everywhere.